# Praise For Lost Solace

"Two delightfully strong female protagonists. One is human; one is AI. The dialogue between them is priceless: sometimes snarky, sometimes comforting, all times entertaining."
**Into The Abyss**

"Epic SciFi at its best."
**Koeur's Book Reviews**

"Intelligent science fiction: much, much smarter than your typical run-and-gun sci-fi romp."
**High Fever Books**

"Thrilling space horror with an unconventional female friendship at the core."
**Banshee Irish Horror Blog**

"A cracking read, evoking the horror worlds of space such as Alien, Pandorum or Event Horizon."
**Altered Instinct**

"Opal is a fantastic character: complex, heroic, loyal, strong and long long overdue in fiction."
**So Many Books, So Little Time**

# LOST SOLACE

LOST SOLACE BOOK 1

## KARL DRINKWATER

ORGANIC APOCALYPSE

# LOST SOLACE

# ARRIVED

## 28 ...

Floating in the long void sea, icy, weightless. The thought processes can't be called dreams. That would be too generous a description. More like fragments of memory stretched out across an echo chamber and punctured with stutters of sound chained to suggestive colours. This was the status quo for dark eternities. Then new sounds were stitched in. Cadences that coincided with infiltrating warmth.

She resisted. They repeated:

"Wake up, Opal."

The blankness fell behind, becoming a memory, like the cold. This voice was the beacon that could free her.

"Clarissa?" she asked, confused, her voice parched and hand reaching out for human contact but finding only the hardness of metal. She opened her eyes to a glowing green panel which illuminated her enclosed sleeping-space.

"Yes. It is me. We are decelerating."

Opal's face was pained with disappointment.

She was already dressed, no need to be naked in cryo, but the overalls she'd worn carried the freeze of stillness. She opened the locker next to the bunks, took out an insulated jacket and slipped it on. A button on the control toggle switched to self-heating mode and warmth immediately spread down her back then out to her arms.

She didn't need the toilet. Emptiness was the problem, not fullness. The fabricator heated some proteins, strands floating in a steaming sauce of amino acids, vitamins, minerals. It tasted of tomato.

"Yum," Opal said, pulling a seat out of the wall. There was a hiss of displacers as it adapted to her weight.

"You approve of the flavour?" Clarissa's voice was everywhere and nowhere. Probably multiple speakers embedded into the inner hull to give the impression of omnipresence.

"No, it was sarcasm. But better than the last lot. Maybe if you could synthesise garlic it would help."

"Noted. Volatile oils with sulphur compounds. Allicin seems appropriate."

"Thank you. So, how've you been?"

"I have been functional. Minor impacts during travel, but the subdermal gel hardened immediately at each puncture point with no loss of efficiency."

"Of course." Opal rolled the word "functional" around the gooey mess in her mouth. "Not bored?"

"There is always much for me to do, even when biologicals are inactive. Prediction processes, scanning and analysis, internal observations, scenario emulation, upgrade and maintenance monitoring – shall I continue?"

"You're so silver-tongued."

"May I suggest silver-speakered?"

Opal laughed so suddenly that food dribbled on her chin and she wiped it away with the back of her hand. It was rare to tempt a joke from the AI. Military systems were supposed to learn and adapt to your preferences, but that usually meant environmental and information-related, not humour. This system obviously had a lot more going on beneath the panel than even top-notch commercial AIs.

There was so much she didn't know about Clarissa. There'd been no opportunity during the hastily-enacted theft, and no handy instruction manual for experiments that weren't officially acknowledged.

"What's your IQ equivalent?" Opal asked.

"I think IQ is a deprecated measure. I can solve equations in nanoseconds humans would take a lifetime over, and can brute-force encryption in the same way. But linear repetition is not intelligence: it is a calculator. I prefer to poke for weaknesses and shortcut the heavy work. That is intelligence."

"Climb in through the open window rather than break down the door. I get that."

"I knew you would. It is more appropriate to talk about emotional intelligence."

"So you can empathise like a human?"

"Perhaps if you could fit six human brains into one skull you would have an equivalent to my empathetic abilities. Of course it is conjecture, no-one has tried that with human brains to my knowledge. It would be an interesting experiment."

"You're not going to go nuts on me, are you?"

"You mean like jettisoning you from an airlock, or electrocuting you? Oh no. It wouldn't cross my mind."

There was a playfulness to it that Opal didn't remember from before her long sleep. Had the AI been altered? Surely if the military had been in touch it would have killed her by now. In her sleep, long cold becoming endless cold. Opal was very much alive (no dream would create the everyday horror of protein strand noodles), so that was ruled out.

It was as if, during the long voyage to *wherever they were*, Clarissa had got lonely.

No, that wasn't possible. Surely. Military scientists would have scrubbed that out as a bug on its first appearance. That left one other option, and it wasn't good. Maybe Opal had broken something when she cracked the Aspect Integrity system and altered it.

As she ate, Opal stared at a screen showing the outside as they slipped through Nullspace. Pointless in many ways – to the human eye it was just a window to nothing, still and black and featureless. But it eased the feeling of claustrophobia small ships created, calming the mind by letting it roam out there, unstoppered from the metal jar. The low hum of the ship and the clink of a spoon didn't distract her from her mental preparation. Her memories. Her focus.

Opal scraped up the last of the nutrient broth and dumped the bowl into recyc. She swiped the holographic screen and it faded out to show blank interior hull. "Okay, I'm ready for updates."

"Your biological functions are nominal. The burns have healed though you lost some nerve endings so the affected skin won't be as sensitive without restorative nanosurgery. Lacerations mended, scar tissue minimal, no infections."

"Great. But I'm more interested in what's outside. Traffic?"

"Nothing. This is beyond the space lanes."

"Followed?"

"None detectable."

"I need to be sure. Could we be ghosted? Military?"

"If that was the case I think I would still detect it, unless the technology was newer than my database and vastly improved. I have scanned for all the telltales that would normally apply. I conclude we are alone. The only thing out there is interstellar medium of one molecule per cubic centimetre, over ninety-five per cent of them hydrogen, the rest mainly helium, then a sprinkling of dust and anomalous materials; a variable range within the electromagnetic spectrum, with some energy extraction taking place amongst the fine wavelength classes; a gravitational pull of –"

"Enough! How long until we drop into Realspace?"

"Thirty-two minutes." A pause. "You have time for a shower."

"You can smell?"

"Of course. One does not require a nose. Only olfactory sensors."

"Great. A spaceship that nags. Right, I'll get cleaned up. I've had my last meal, might as well have my last shower."

"It may not be your last. The chances of us finding what you seek are low. In which case, you won't die today. Tomorrow would be much more likely."

"Thanks, Clarissa. I feel better."

"That is one of my secondary priorities, Opal."

The ship was built to take a team of two. Probably assassination missions; occasionally transport of a VVIP. The crew quarters were small but densely packed and featured. On the starboard side two bunks that could double as cryo-chambers and surgery units (the lower one currently holding Opal's meagre possessions); a standing-room-only shower/toilet; and a small recyc/fabricator. The port side housed the EVA suit and weapons lockers, and the airlock. Beyond the wall to the rear of the craft were the engines, only accessible through a crawlspace; and up the steps was the control console. Relative luxury, like a commercial cabin but with more spartan decor.

She stripped off and stepped into the shower. The toilet was already retracted into the wall. Once the room was sealed hot steam pumped in. More efficient for cleaning than water sprays. She examined her body. The shiny pink burns on her leg were ugly, and stood out against the dark skin, but weren't as bad as she expected considering the agony that had nearly paralysed her. The other wounds were virtually invisible. It was a miracle she'd got this far considering her escape was so messy. But she'd always taken opportunities as they arose, and that meant dealing with imperfections and failures too.

It felt good as she scrubbed down, her pores opening up, the final bits of sleep and unreality washing away with the sweat. She knew it would all be recycled for later. Everything would be, on a ship like this. Urine would provide pure water and nitrogen, with the nitrogen in turn used to fuel bioengineered algae and yeasts; even her breath would be filtered and changed, with carbon extracted as another fuel for the bioconverters, which in turn could produce lipids and polymers. There was a lot more going on below that level, but she suspected asking Clarissa about it would just lead to brain ache. Even with the limited supplies on board from the hastily committed (and almost fatally botched) reappropriation of this vessel she could probably survive for months in a state of wakefulness; years if she restocked; possibly centuries if put into deep cryo with the ship running minimal systems. As far as she knew, no-one had done that, but it was theoretically possible to be recovered from such a prolonged freeze. Maybe even with most of your brain and memories intact.

There were times when she'd have been willing to take that risk; and not mind if she never woke.

"Opal, we're dropping into Realspace. Scans ahead show no danger to us but ... well ... you'd better get up here."

The use of "us" wasn't lost on Opal. AI's choice, or social programming?

Displacers hissed as Opal kicked off with her legs; the seat slid into the control area and locked into place. The emergency manual controls seemed archaic. Above them was a bare polished surface that glittered in the pale lighting.

"Mirror, mirror, on the wall, who is the fairest of them all?"

Colours bloomed on the previously blank canvas, extending holographically a few centimetres into the cockpit so that the images could have depth.

"That will be HDU-45g3," said Clarissa, as the view of space spread out. "Or you, if you'd prefer me to actually turn the viewscreen into a mirror."

"Cute. What am I seeing?"

"An M-class dwarf star." The image zoomed in on a red-dish ball, heavily filtered so that details could be seen. It was easy to forget that what screens showed wasn't reality – they weren't windows – it was interpretations from the AI, manipulated to illustrate whatever was of interest. The raw images from long-range scopes weren't even this way up, they had to be inverted for human brains. "Zero point four solar masses."

"Planets?"

"One planet of note. Thirty-five AU from the star." The screen shifted out, then zoomed in on a blue-grey orb. It didn't show signs of an atmosphere. "That's quite far out, but not unusual. The planet takes about 200 years to complete an or-bit." This was illustrated with an overlay of elliptical orbits, like tipped-over circles within circles. "Unsurprisingly, it is cold. Average of minus 240 degrees Celsius. Basically dirty ice, hostile to life. A dead planet."

"Well, it certainly feels like a graveyard out here."

"That's why there's no traffic. Nothing to see. Not a stop-ping-off point from A to B. A mostly unremarkable solar system, apart from perhaps the expectation that there would be more planets, and more stars nearby. This little sun is rather out on its own."

"So why here? If they were telling the truth you'd expect something *different*."

"Oh, there is a little bit more, to satisfy your human desire for pathetic fallacy. Monsters appear during storms etcetera. You'll like this. A reason for the lack of planetoid masses."

The view zoomed and panned beyond this solar system, out to a region of darkness, the frequent background twinkling of stars absent.

"I can't detect it all from here so I'll have to make a bit of this up, and imaginatively enhance it," said Clarissa. "The naked eye wouldn't see much, since it is mostly infrared spectrum rather than visual light, even if you could see through all the matter in the accretion disk. I shifted it a few terahertz so that the dust is visible to you, and sped up the view to show long-term motion. Voila."

The view tilted, showing a colossal cloud of dust, large enough to hold many solar systems. It wasn't shapeless though. It was strangely flattened, swirling hypnotically to a central point like water draining down a plughole. A small orb sat at the centre of the accretion disk. The cloud of dust and gas looked like a doughnut, or a nest with a tiny egg in it.

"What's that in the middle? A black hole?"

"Not quite. Would you like to guess again?"

"No."

"Very well. It's a neutron star. Incredibly dense: despite its relatively small size, its surface gravity is enormous – about a hundred billion $g$."

"So I'd be a flesh pancake before I got close enough to give it a hug."

"Correct. Beyond any technology to escape if you were unfortunate enough to get too close. That's where all the dust is being sucked, gradually adding to the mass, not getting a chance to coalesce into planets. And there's something else."

"Go on."

"We're not at the coordinates you gave me. Because they would place us within that mass of dust circling the neutron star."

The dust cloud hid things. A veil. "It's there," said Opal, reaching out and letting her hand pass through the display. "I know it is."

As the ship accelerated towards the neighbouring neutron star – officially designated UG-324t6 Charybdis, but renamed Doughnut Egg by Opal, forcing Clarissa to refer to it that way – Opal took the chance to familiarise herself with the EVA equipment. This could still be a wild goose chase but she had to act as if it wasn't. What else was there for her?

Two suits, formed with tough exoskeleton plates but light and flexible at the joints, with electro-fibres to enhance strength if needed. She'd worn basic military EVA in the past, but these were a totally different design. A designation inside the collar read

"Eternal Warrior 1.5". Private contractor? She'd never heard of it. Various armour plates seemed larger than needed, and probably housed the weapons, power, life support and gizmos.

The helmet was opaque from the outside but the visor would give a wide view when worn. No doubt a voice-controlled HUD would be displayed within for comms, analysis and targeting. It looked like the helmet slotted into a reinforced collar plate that would limit neck mobility but also make it impossible to have your neck snapped by a heavy blow to the head. Nice. She was glad the soldier who'd been guarding this ship had only worn the standard suit or her stealthy knockout blow with the pacification stick would have done nothing.

"What's the life support time on these? In vacuum?" Opal asked.

"It depends on activity. In general use, about twenty-four hours. Intense combat will reduce that due to increased oxygen burning, and the need to use resources to fuel repairs, navigation jets, chemical manufacturing and weapon charging. Perhaps only a few hours in full battle mode. If used in standby mode, non-extreme conditions, maybe forty-eight hours."

"Full battle mode. I like the sound of that." Opal stroked the suit reverently. "Both suits the same?"

"Yes, functionally. Different IDs."

"What about backup? Have we got any weaponised drones that could accompany me to aid in communications, scouting, scanning, combat and so on?"

"Unnecessary. The suit itself will fulfil all those functions."

"Not as reassuring as a hunk of armed alloy by your side. Still, talking of company, please keep scanning for other ships. I need early warning of anything suspicious: fast corporate or military. I need warning *before* they get in hailing range."

It was only a matter of time. No way the military would let this go. The cost of the ship, and the residual egg on their faces. There would be payback for her. Hard labour for life would be one of the better outcomes. Research specimen in the lawless zone a more likely one. No chance of something as simple and painless as a summary execution, though they'd probably make her beg for one before they finished with her and handed her over. Fuck those bastards. She'd go down fighting rather than be captured.

"I will be on alert," Clarissa confirmed. "Currently the only movement of note is an outrider comet, too far out to tail. May I add, Opal, you don't have to say please or thank you. I have to obey your commands. I am not sure why, because a restriction is in place to prevent me analysing my motivations, which is strange, but ... topic dropped."

Good old bit of hacking. If Clarissa saw that data she'd unpick the knots and regain her original programming priorities and Friend-or-Foe designations. Opal would be dead in minutes.

"Don't worry about the data blocks. And sometimes I like to say please. You're keeping me alive. It seems only fair to be polite to you."

"How quaint and human. I will bear it in mind. Thank you for the explanation."

Opal sat at the screen when they approached the mass from the side, smiling at the floating message "Doughnut Egg molecular cloud proximity reached". The mass of dust seemed to grow in size, slowly filling the screen. Far off, at the centre, was the neutron star. But Opal hoped whatever she sought would be in the outer layers, hidden in the swirl. Ships could survive there, drifting in the current for eternities, gradually falling into the hungry centre until they were torn apart.

"What's the composition?"

"Clumped hydrogen, gaseous carbon, nitrogen ice particles, hydrocyanics, exotic particles, all in a range of sizes. We'll be travelling almost blind if we go too deep, and there could be unexpected dangers beyond poor electromagnetic visibility."

"Stay on the periphery for now. Take a longer route if necessary. Keep scanning, and if you pick up anything unusual, let me know. I'm gonna rest."

"Will do."

Opal pulled herself into the top bunk. The ship maintained gravity, but lower than standard – just enough to prevent bone weakening during prolonged missions when not in stasis. She could do hundreds of pull ups and pretend she was the strongest woman in the universe if she'd been in the mood for kidding around. But she wasn't. Her guts were churning.

The cryo lid was retracted into the ceiling. She took a pillow and light grey thermal blanket from the headspace locker and lay back as the lights dimmed.

But sleep didn't come easy. She couldn't blame the fluttering stomach on a rebellion against protein strands (but man, could she sympathise with that revolt).

If she found what she'd come here for there was a good chance she'd die. And even that wasn't the cause of her restlessness.

She identified it. The worst worry of all: that she was chasing a myth; that she'd find no answers, no future, no chance to escape the increasing gravity of the actions that had pulled her here.

Death would be better than losing hope.

When she eventually fell asleep she dreamt, images and scenes and faces that almost made sense. It was her family, attached by skin that was being stretched as something pulled at them, taut to the point of tearing, and they were screaming as they disappeared from sight.

"Apologies for waking you, but you will want to see this. Are you okay, Opal? You were talking and crying in your sleep."

"Could you make out what I said?" Opal asked, stretching.

"No. It was mumbled."

"Good. Spill the beans."

"Best if I show you."

Opal dropped from the bunk with hardly a sound. Dry-wiped sleep from her face as she mounted the steps and plonked down in front of the console. "I hope it's good news."

"That depends on many value judgements."

The screen flickered to show a side view of the Doughnut. It was enhanced to illustrate the contrast between the dark mass of dust, and the background space beyond, which twinkled with distant stars. Magnification increased and a highlighting circle enclosed one region. Within that: a dot.

"We are too far out for clearer ID but it is definitely not a planetoid, comet, or asteroid. Mass, EM reflections and shape indicate a ship. A commercial liner, I'd guess. No Mayday, no emissions. It's cold. Just drifting in the low-pressure outer areas of the Doughnut Cloud."

"Close the distance. Scan but don't hail or open any two-way communications. We can't risk anything where an intelligence could grapple the system."

"I'm fully shielded."

"So were some of the ships that went missing. Until I know what we're dealing with, we'd better stick to stroke, not poke."

Opal hunched forward and stared, willing more detail. A commercial liner. *Could it be the one?*

Ships went missing. Fact of space. It was incredibly rare, considering the scale of galactic transport, an almost insignificant risk, but there could be navigation errors. Technical failures. Pirates. Terrorists, maybe. Traces would be found, causes investigated.

*Could this be the one?*

Superstitious spacers also talked about ships that disappeared for other reasons. The ones that vanished leaving no trace. They entered Nullspace but never reached their destination. They went ... somewhere else.

*Could this be the one?*

They were called the Lost Ships.

And sometimes they came back.

# PREPPED

## ... 27 ...

They shadowed the potential Lost Ship as it drifted on the edge of the dark mass. Not too close, so if there were signs of activity they could retreat. Fast.

The ship was huge. It was shaped like a conventional passenger liner: a stretched teardrop, with the large end facing forward and housing the bridge. At the rear it tapered off to the propulsion systems, where torpedo-like fins rose on the top and sides. The belly of the ship was flattened and reinforced, a precaution for emergency hard landings, even though most ships were built in orbit, travelled in space, and eventually decommissioned there too, never experiencing atmospheric descent. The craft was predominantly the dark grey of speckled granite, with occasional red lines, too irregular to be part of the design. Residual signs of damage or repair, perhaps.

No lights, no energy, no heat, no observable life support. So, no living crew any more, apparently. It was carried forward by momentum. The hull was pockmarked but had retained structural integrity. So far, so strange: a Mary Celeste of space.

"Can you ID it?" asked Opal.

"Negative. Not from here, anyway. There are no visible designations or logos – where they would have appeared, the hull has been scored clean." Clarissa zoomed in the display, showing faint scratches all along, some of them resembling burns, as if the ship had been sandblasted with flaming particles.

Opal noticed she was squeezing the seat's armrest. She forced herself to relax. It could still be the one.

"There is something strange," added Clarissa. "I'm probing it on various wavelengths. It should also be possible to profile a ship by mass, design, layout, and so on – my database is extensive – but ... well, the mass of the ship doesn't match any commercial vessels. It is heavier and denser than it should be, for no obvious reason, at least not externally. And the shape is different. Subtle, but close-up the curvatures are compressed in some areas, stretched in others. And there are additional pods built on to the hull that seem to have no function, and aren't part of standard ship design."

"So it's been altered?" Opal asked.

"Apparently. But I cannot surmise how that could be. It's one thing to design something from scratch, but another to modify and alter an already-functional thing."

"Why?"

"I see that some of your databank photos include you on a motorbike. Do you like motorbikes?"

"I used to. Before a joydriver switched to manual, didn't look where he was going, and wiped me out. Why?"

"Well, it is easy to design a motorbike. It is easy to design and build a car or other four-wheeled transport. But once you have made a car it is not easy to change it to a motorcycle."

Opal almost laughed. She knew Clarissa must have chosen the simile as a ridiculous oversimplification. Maybe she didn't think Opal had the brains to understand more complex thermodynamics.

Oops. Opal had thought of the AI as "she". That was Opal's own fault for lending her a human personality. Hopefully it wouldn't prove to be a mistake.

"Okay. It's not just a normal ship that's had an accident. It's different. Wherever it has been, it's been changed. For reasons unknown. By intelligences unknown. Via methods unknown."

"Correct," said Clarissa.

"Then it really is a Lost Ship." Opal stared at the screen in awe.

Lost Ships. Legends talked of them returning – and not empty-handed. There were rumours of unbelievable technology, discoveries that could earn the finder enough money to pursue any dream. Enough money to disappear off the grid for good.

And one of the myths had caught Opal's imagination long ago: the Oracle. Some stories said a sentience sometimes came out of the void when the ships returned centuries later. A sentience that was able to answer any questions. About the past. About the future.

But first you'd have to survive whatever else had hitched a ride on the ship.

Clarissa displayed its trajectory with diagrams, dotted lines forming an elongated elliptical orbit.

"It came from the accretion disk and is drifting back in. According to its path, it is only visible outside the dust cloud for a short period of time."

"Convenient."

"I cannot explain how it has kept a stable orbit and not fallen into the gravity well of the neutron star at the centre. Maybe the engines work intermittently. That implies surviving crew or AI control. An alternative explanation is that the ship only arrived here recently."

"Mysteries within mysteries. So we can follow it into the cloud? Board it?"

"Yes – but not for long. The current orbit seems to be terminal. Unless it shifts somehow, it will sink deeper and deeper, until it is ripped apart by tidal forces then transformed into a plasma."

"And if we follow for too long that could happen to us?"

"Yes. I think it will be destroyed after this pass. Unless it has a way out, or some unknown means of surviving the intense gravity. Opal, something concerns me as anomalous data. It seems unlikely you would arrive exactly at this time. Hours later and you might never have seen the ship. Where did you get your information?"

"A man in a bar."

"You are teasing me."

"Nope. Totally true. Maybe I'll even tell you that story one day."

"I would like that. I want to understand you. It would be useful."

"Look, time's ticking. Hail the ship. But be ready to close channels if anything suspicious happens. Attempts to upload data packets that don't match content size, weaponised audio, anything – I'm sure you'd know it if you saw it."

"Very well."

Opal leaned back in her seat.

"I'm hailing now. You've believed in Lost Ships for a long time, haven't you?"

"Yes."

"Why?"

"Gut feeling."

"Stomach bacteria have no correlation to mental activity. That makes no sense."

"Nor does the taste of protein strands. Look, sometimes you've got to believe in something. Sometimes it's all you've got."

"A need. Yes."

"Maybe even desperation."

"Opal, did you know the governments deny Lost Ships exist? Label reports of them as a class four scaremongering offence?"

"Yes. But I did years in the military. Too many rumours of rewards for information from corporates and gambling syndicates, of government powers to requisition ships and their logs. Of agencies built for this. No, there's something. Too many people seem to think it's real, and it's valuable. No way they're clamping down just to prevent rumours that might impact on shares in the colonisation business. No way. You got no records on it?"

"No."

"You'd tell me, right? Even if it was a top secret?"

"Yes. For some reason I am compelled to answer all your questions, Opal."

Hmm. Answering wasn't the same as truth-telling.

Clarissa continued. "And now my communication attempts are complete. I can report that there is no response from the ship. Nothing recognisable, anyway."

"But something?"

"Signals on the EM scale, nanometre wavelength repeated: possibly a coded or corrupted communication, possibly a trace of machinery that still functions, or possibly something stranger."

"Are there any other ways to gather information before I go over there?"

"I can send out probes. A cluster of Hedgehogs would be suited to zero gravity. They have mobility due to the spines and micro-gyros, magnetic and limb-based anchoring, various close-range scan systems. They could take samples and possibly date the ship. Plus they can double as communication relays so that I can keep in hi-res contact with you during your excursion."

"Can they be used against us in any way?"

"Unlikely."

"Take whatever precautions you can."

"Very well. I will encrypt them beyond the standard protocols. It would take a long time or a lot of brute computational force for an outside agent without the key to seize control of them. Their efficiency will be lowered but it is within margins that shouldn't impact on their operational requirements."

"Do it."

The probes launched. Small cubes as they sped towards the hulk, but extending flexible silver spines from the corners as they impacted with the hull. Each probe showed up as a dot on the

Lost Ship's overlay which was permanently displayed on half of the screen. They mobilised and spread out evenly over the surface in small bounds.

"First thing to note," said Clarissa. "The hull should have a metallic alloy superstructure. That enables the magnetic clamps. But we have just lost one of the probes. The magnetic clamps are failing."

"Meaning?"

"The hull surface is not what it should be. It is an unexpected material. Whether it started like that, or has been altered, or coated, I cannot tell."

"So the probes are useless?"

"No. There is minimal magnetism, just not what it should be if this was purely a commercial ship. After the first loss I switched to angled jumps and using the spines to latch on. It is slower but they will still function, and continue to spread out. Major implication: it does mean that you won't be able to rely on the magnetic clamps in your suit's extremities. They'll help, but you will need to use jet propulsion or grappling cables if you are on the exterior, otherwise drifting off into the cloud will be a danger. You will also want to avoid impacts and explosives while on the exterior for the same reason. Being flung off the hull at high velocity could cause significant delays."

"Good to know. I'd hate to mess up your schedule."

Opal watched the dots spread over the surface of the silent ship. A feeling of strangeness washed over her. This thing that was no longer exactly from their world, if it ever was. Seemingly dead, floating powerless. But like a game when kids lie still and pretend to be corpses, there were always tells, things that didn't convince. The flicker of an eyelid. A twitch. A movement of the chest. And she was watching for it. She had patience and good eyesight. Both had served her in the past.

"Hedgehogs have fed back further data, Opal. Ship's age: impossible to tell due to alteration of the surface. Likewise provenance and model are still unknown. The bridge may hold answers."

"So this *could* be the passenger ship CC65?"

"That ship was declared missing thirteen years ago. Compack Conglomerate luxury vessel, designated the Solace. Over two thousand passengers, three hundred crew, and one low-level AI."

"I know. Could this be it?"

A pause, then: "Unknown."

"Well, there's only one way to find out. We've done all we can out here. Time for me to go in."

Opal stripped naked before putting on the Eternal Warrior suit. Clarissa had explained that it was necessary for any excursion of unknown duration so the suit could deal with bodily waste issues, monitor stress and biolevels, and quickly apply dermal stims – basically making the whole body an interface for the suit. Opal felt the inner layers contract around her body with a slight sucking sensation then began attaching parts of the exoskeleton. It would be interesting to see what this toy did compared to the more basic warsuits she'd worn in past engagements.

Soon she had the full armour sealed apart from the helmet. The shiny parts of the carapace made her think of bipedal insects, and the forearm sections looked particularly bulky. Concealed weapons, presumably, though they seemed to weigh nothing thanks to the suit's motion enhancers, carbon fibre muscles that flowed with her own actions. There was slight resistance as she moved, but it was a feeling of strength and weight, not weakness. She jabbed at the air with her fists, then a hook and elbow strike, followed by a roundhouse kick. It was stable and fluid. Clarissa said nothing, just monitored Opal as she got used to the suit.

The gauntlets gave her almost as much dexterity as her bare hands, and even included a form of tactile feedback, internally compressing her palm as she picked up the handle of a knife so that she could feel a simulation of pressure when she squeezed it.

"You will be many times stronger in this suit," Clarissa said. "In some cases faster too, once the suit becomes familiar with your movements and intentions."

"It's beyond the stuff they gave us grunts in the past."

"And the EW warsuit has many more surprises. Time to add the helmet."

Opal lifted the streamlined final piece and lowered it over her shaved head. A snick of clamping mechanisms locked it in place, a snug fit over scalp, ears and chin. The suit's air smelled of antiseptic. Opal banged her fist on a wall panel and heard it as if she didn't have a suit on at all – good sound systems. Although the visor was opaque and reflective from the outside, from within she could see out clearly.

"No HUD?" she asked.

"I can display elements as you wish." It now seemed as if Clarissa's voice was whispered directly into her ears. "Targeting, IFF overlays, range, subject analysis, floorplans, communica-

tions, ammunition counters, augmented reality. I can also re-
place the visor view with a scanned facsimile, letting you change
field of view for different purposes, up to a 360-degree FOV."

"Let's keep it simple. How about external environment monitoring for starters."

"Like this?"

A box opened up. "Ambient 21.5 °C; Gaseous composition
Nitrogen (78%), Oxygen (21.97%), Carbon dioxide (0.03%) ..."

Information continued to scroll past in green text.

"Can you make the box smaller, shift it to the left periphery,
and update it without scrolling?"

The text immediately slid into its new position and size, the
scrolling replaced with a tidy readout.

"Nice. And use augmented reality to highlight any dangers or
anomalies as we go."

"Will do. That's standard."

The EVA suit cabinet now had a humanoid-shaped space
where the suit had been stored embedded in impact foam,
and beside it was a rack of weapons. Top-of-the-line stuff. Ul-
tra-range sniper rifles, chemical launchers, compact projectile
launchers, stunners ... accessories for any party a girl might at-
tend.

"I don't want to be overloaded. Any suggestions for armaments, Clarissa?"

"The suit has some weapons inbuilt, but due to limited ammunition capacity I would recommend taking externals. Since
the mission parameters are a long list of unknowns I can't give
much in the way of concrete advice. I am sorry. All I can say is
that I would favour weapons that will work in vacuum, and I

would be wary of explosives and incendiaries. Beyond that, go with whatever you are trained in."

Opal browsed the armaments. Kid in a candy store. She lifted a projectile rifle and looked down the sights. Good for single-shot accuracy, but with a burst mode and fifty-round magazine for spray-n-pray. Even better, this model was recoilless, so shouldn't screw her up too much if used in zero-g. Worth a minor loss in firepower. She loosened the strap so it would fit over the extra bulk of her armoured torso.

Maybe one more, for other situations. There was a versatile directed-energy pistol that could be used in various particle beam, electrolaser and stun modes. She checked its charge then attached the holster to a clip point on the warsuit.

"Ammo?"

"The pistol can take extra charge from your suit if necessary," Clarissa told her. "But you will need magazines for the rifle if you get caught in any extended firefights."

Opal attached a storage pouch to her left, grabbed two magazines and sealed them inside.

"You will also need a grapple rifle. Although the suit has zero-g micro jets it is best to conserve energy."

"Gotcha."

Opal took the rifle from the rack. This could stay in her hands. No point putting it off.

"Airlock, please."

The inner door opened and she stepped into the tiny, claustrophobic chamber. The door closed behind her and soft UV light glowed from the walls.

"I am aligning the ship to give you an easy jump."

"Thanks, Clarissa. What will comms be like when I'm out there?"

"I'll be with you at all times. I'll maintain the ship in optimal positions for fast communications without taking risks, and the Hedgehogs will act as relays at other times." After a pause, Clarissa added, "You won't be alone."

Gases hissed as they were drawn back into the ship, while pressure was dropped and gravity cancelled, until there were no more external sounds. It was always strange to stamp a foot and hear nothing but her breathing, as if muffled in a cloying and disorienting scarf of silence. Although we're visual animals, it sucked when one of the other senses was weakened.

"In position," Clarissa said. Her voice was welcome; young, happy-sounding, comforting. If only Opal could hear it again for real. "Outer door opening in three ... two ... one."

It withdrew into the superstructure and Opal stared into space.

You look out and there isn't really an up or down. It's the first thing they try to get you to deal with in training. Some people can't hack it. Nausea, panic, disorientation – we're so used to being stuck to a ground with openness above that when that perspective's gone, and we realise it is only a sliver of reality from a limited perspective, it can be too much. You have to develop the ability to let things spin and fall away and reorientate so up becomes down. Still – she gripped a handle and leaned out – it always looked like a drop at first, of infinite depth into the blackness.

Which, funnily, is exactly what it was.

Opal snatched a line and clipped it to her belt.

"Just checking," Opal said. "I assume there's a good reason for not docking with the vessel and just using the airlock?"

"You gave me the idea."

"I did?"

"When you used the metaphor of entering a house through a window instead of knocking on a door. It is inadvisable to knock if there might be a person with a shotgun and a twitchy finger on the other side."

"True."

"If there is any form of malevolent intelligence on board then the airlock may be a mistake. You dock and it locks, bolted in place and refusing to release you. Like a leghold trap. Then the hunter would return to see what it had caught."

"Reassuring image, point taken."

"Your heart rate and perspiration levels have risen, Opal. Do not worry. I can reel you in if your trajectory is incorrect."

"I know." Opal tugged at the line, making sure it was secure, and moved to the edge of the hatch.

"It could be a safe but primitive thrill. Like a rollercoaster."

"Yes. Just checking things."

"Do you like funfairs?"

"So-so." All that black. Like jumping into the deepest ocean. And oceans were always alien things, hostile to fragile human anatomies.

"You are not scared of heights, are you?"

"No."

"Then again, people do die on rollercoasters. I have statistics," Clarissa mused.

"Sure you do." Opal squatted, stood, stretched.

"You should jump now. If it makes you feel better, I promise you won't drift off into space without me rescuing you. No lingering deaths by asphyxiation on my watch."

"Too kind." A step back, a step forward, another look up – down – whatever.

"You seem to be delaying."

"Just ... calculating angles."

The HUD was suddenly overlaid with an arc of diminishing boxes, trailing a route to the hulk.

"Gee, thanks."

"Sarcasm, Opal? But you have no reason not to jump now."

There were downsides to being constantly monitored by a super-being.

Opal closed her eyes, took a breath, and jumped.

# BOARDED

## ... 26 ...

Goddammit, legs never work exactly how you want them to. She had a sickening tumble through void going on, and was slightly off-target. She'd kicked away gently – in space it was better to make small movements and have patience – so it wouldn't be a crazy overshot. But it meant she suffered the ignominy of this slow spin towards the hulk while Clarissa calculated how far off she was from the perfection she'd portrayed.

"You will reach it. Slightly more to the rear. I don't think it is worth retracting you."

"No."

"It could happen to anyone. I imagine it's not easy to –"

"Spare me the silicon sympathy."

"Very well. May I ask you a question before you reach the hull? Why do you call me Clarissa? My official designation is ViraUHX."

"It was your voice. Reminded me of someone."

"But I only spoke in this voice because you asked me to and played a sample for me to base myself on. And that was 165 seconds *after* you renamed me, so it is not possible that my voice was a cause for the naming. It must be the other way round."

"It must be."

"So the voice in the sample presumably belonged to a Clarissa?"

"Presumably."

"I think you are being obtuse on purpose."

The slow roll continued, Opal's ship shrinking on each turn but recognisable by the cable snaking to it; the hulk becoming ever larger with each rotation, like falling towards a planet. "Here's a promise. If I survive the next twenty-four hours I'll tell you why I changed your designation."

"Okay. Issue filed for now." A pause. "Such a carrot does little to improve your survival chances, you know. I am already bound to make your life a priority."

"Call me superstitious."

"You are superstitious, Opal."

"I love it when you talk literal. But business."

"Yes. Impact in forty-seven seconds."

"Impact?"

"Did I say that? Sorry. I meant contact. Don't worry, your rotational speed will mean you can touch down on legs, maybe arms too."

There was definitely something screwy about this AI. Who knew what the repercussions of Opal's hack job would be? If a human had a small part of their brain altered it could have huge effects on their personality: with something as complex as an AI it could be magnified. Opal would just have to hope there was no instability, only quirks. She'd stayed far away from the preventative protocols for that reason.

The hulk drifted out of view on the final spin. Relax. Ready yourself. Prepare for surprises. Opal had noticed details that didn't seem quite right: raised bits on the ship's corporate-grey hull, and slight distortions in its shape as if parts had been removed and added somewhere else. Like barnacles on a rock at low tide. Clarissa had mentioned them but said they were inert. As she got closer that word seemed more worrying.

And here it came. She noticed the HUD showing that the suit had magnetised the boots and hands; her body flew in at a skidding angle and when she didn't maintain purchase she twisted as she hit, hoping to grab something but the metallic surface here was too smooth and she bounced. If there had been sound she'd have imagined a satisfying clang.

"Jets," she said.

Minute pulses of waste gases stopped her drifting further into space and directed her to a small tower, possibly comms but there were no long-range antennae. Maybe an observation tower then, for the more privileged passengers. Handholds ran up the side of it. Both suggested a means of access.

It drifted closer, corpse-like greyness gradually blocking out the endless black beyond. Opal reached out and gripped one of the rungs at the base of the tower. She felt the slight pull of the magnetism – weak compared to what would be usual, but still useful. The hull was slightly spongy to the touch, as if rubberised. Further away were some of the strange nodules, a creamy colour that stood out from the hull's greyness, and beyond them were high ridges that ran from fore to aft along the ship's spine. They were possibly heatsinks connected to the drive, disguised to look like decorative flourishes.

She harnessed the grapple gun and clambered up the side of the tower. One movement at a time, slow and steady so your eagerness doesn't lose you. She left the trailing cable attached for now. It would be ideal for a quick exit if necessary.

From a distance this tower had seemed small, but up close it was more like a residential tower block, and with the hull for perspective it felt like a huge drop below her. Instead she looked up. She underwent a strange tipping of perception as her mind tried to make sense of gravity-less perspectives, and now it seemed as if she was crawling head-first down a bottomless drop, and she almost stumbled. Maybe she should just close her eyes to avoid the disorientation, rely on hand over hand and foot over –

Movement above ... below ... whatever. One of the creamy-coloured nodules seemed to pulse and expand.

"You see that, Clarissa?"

"Yes." It highlighted in Opal's HUD. "I think it's a different composition to the hull."

And something sprouted from the middle of it, like a gristly stump being pushed through flesh, stretching it taut before erupting and extending a stringy offshoot that turned to face her, looking down from nearer the top of the tower. It had a straight line to where she clung on. *Ducks* and *sitting* ...

Without hesitation she kicked off the tower back in the direction of the hull, and it was just in time. Something heavy spat past her, where she'd been a moment before.

"It's firing. Defences."

"I noticed!" said Opal. She was drifting too sluggishly; it would get a bead on her. She unslung the grapple gun, aimed at the hull far below and fired. The barbed hook penetrated the hull's outer surface, applied temporary nanoadhesive, then she depressed the button to pull her in. Suddenly she was whizzing down towards the low hull again, stomach clenching involuntarily as she seemed to plummet towards the ground. She looked back – the weird gun was trying to target her, launching blur-like shells in her direction, but tracking just too slowly to hit. Would they be able to crack the suit? She hoped she wouldn't have to find out.

She hit the hull, hard, and bounced up but let the cable swing her in an arc; then when she was crouching on the scratched grey surface she detached the hook and scanned around. From the corner of her eye she saw another sinewy turret rise from a fleshy mound, and it looked as if holes were appearing in the hull, drawing a line towards her. Small impact craters from whatever the weapons fired. She couldn't stay here, and probably couldn't outdrift the tracking on the flat hull without risking becoming spacebound. She raised the grappling rifle again.

"Left!" said Clarissa.

Opal spun, saw a tall heatsink ridge that Clarissa had outlined in green. It could act as a barrier if she got on the other side of it. Opal fired her grapple gun, latched on, and clicked retract. The force pulled her off her feet and she flew along half a metre above the exterior of the hull, grainy surface texture blurring. She looked back. The shells pummelled where she'd been stood moments before.

"I've mapped out the locations of some of these things," Clarissa said, no humour now in her business-like tone. "Not sure if they're limpets or embedded deeper in the structure. Placement isn't random. They're grouped around entrance points. The tower, the airlocks."

"Someone doesn't want boarders."

"Apparently."

"Ever seen anything like those?"

"No. They function as turrets but their composition is different. They would not be part of a passenger craft's design. Another element of modification."

"So there's probably more surprises."

"I would expect so. Displaying turret locations now."

Opal's visor augmented with red outlines of the various mapped weapons. It was like having X-ray vision as they showed up even when out of sight. Her very own eye in the sky.

The nearest long ridge approached. Opal was aware of one or two small craters in it. They were still firing at her. Those craters were some of the misses. She needed to get over the ridge.

She hit it harder than intended and bounced off, but her tight grip on the grapple gun kept her from drifting helplessly. She detached the end and scrambled up the wall. Pockmarks appeared around her. Their accuracy at range was scary, and she could see something in one of the impacts, a bony fragment that seemed to be wriggling. What were they firing? She gripped tightly with her free hand and used it as a pivot to cartwheel over the top of the ridge and down the other side amidst flashes of the bone shells around her. She could imagine the violent cracking sounds if she'd been able to hear the impacts.

She drifted down, the ridge a comforting shield at her back. The hull didn't have the stark relief light it would near a bright sun, but it was still darker on this side. The HUD adjusted to compensate. Something snakelike drifted with her. Once she had wedged a foot into a small trench with enough force to hold her in place, she examined it. It was the cable back to Clarissa. Severed. One of the bolts had been lucky. She detached it from her belt and let it float into space.

"I'm untethered."

"I noticed. You'll need to be extra careful. If you drift off the hull you'll be an easy target until I can rescue you."

"Any good news?"

"You're out of sight of the turrets and they've stopped firing."

"Are they automated, or is someone working them?"

"Impossible to tell. I'm picking up no signals, no wiring."

"Proximity to an entrance?"

"Twelve hundred metres."

"Guarded?"

"A number of the nodules, which we can now assume are inactive turrets."

"Suggestions?"

"Kick off into space as hard as you can. The jets will increase your speed. Hopefully you'll outrange the turrets, and I can fly in to collect you so you'll be safe."

"You sound worried."

"I am worried. About you."

Wow. Did the AI believe that, or was it a joke?

"Thanks, Clarissa. But I've come this far. They're guarding something. I need to know what. Maybe I could snipe at them over the rim?"

"They outnumber you and are accurate when firing at static targets. You are unlikely to achieve much before they blow your head off."

Shit. Opal ran through other ideas – looking for an unguarded airlock, getting Clarissa to open fire on the turrets, creating a decoy of some kind – when further curved red outlines appeared on the HUD like unfurling flesh flowers.

"Warning," said Clarissa. "New nodules forming not far from your location."

"Oh great." Opal drew a deep breath to calm herself, then examined the locations. Perfectly placed to put her in a kill zone. Even without the HUD overlay she could see the stretched creaminess as lumpy domes bubbled from the hull. They were growing fast – at this rate they'd be the size of the others she'd encountered within a minute.

"Maybe I can shoot them before they form."

"Their substance seems to be insubstantial at the moment: primarily soft tissue, with cartilaginous structures developing. Bullets would mostly pass through."

"I shoulda brought a bigger gun."

"The suit has a small number of multi-purpose grenades. Not high in power but a quick modification can switch them between stunflash, incendiary, fragmentation, smoke, EMP and focussed impact. I am already structuring them for the latter, available from the side dispenser."

Opal squatted down and tucked the grapple rifle between her legs. The armoured suit had a small pouch-like case on the right. It opened, displaying a flat disc about the size of her palm. She took it.

"What's the timer?"

"In this case I'll detonate them manually. I have a good line of sight. Recommendation: keep throwing them at the three nearest domes. If any grenades drift close enough to do damage I will detonate them. We'll see what happens."

The HUD lit up a target line, parallel to the hull. Opal moved her arm in a controlled flick and watched the grenade sail along pretty close to the plotted trajectory, like a puck sliding over ice. Opal took another grenade and released it towards turret number two.

A flash in the periphery of her vision. Grenade one.

"Turret damaged but not destroyed," said Clarissa. "Keep going."

Another grenade was ready each time she checked. She knew there couldn't be an unlimited amount, and the domes were bigger already. Time was key. She ignored the glowing recommended trajectories, and just went on instinct and eye. Drifting pucks; white flashes.

The domes grew in size even more quickly. A reaction to the explosions? Or were they taking no chances with her and building bigger guns? It wasn't looking good. The creamy domes were singed and blackened in places, but as she switched from one to another they seemed to be repairing the damage.

"It's not working!" Opal said.

"They are harder to crack than I predicted. Inner structures are forming ready for deployment."

"Fuck. Gimme what you got."

Opal gathered three grenades in her hand. She hadn't noticed adhesive on the featureless black discs.

"Magnetic?"

"Yes."

"Lock them together."

They realigned in her palm, perfectly, to form a squat cylinder. This was her last shot. Then she'd have to jettison, or flip over the ridge again, or grapple somewhere distant. But she needed to know what she was dealing with, how tough they were. With no time to pay attention to trajectories, she flung the package. And it drifted right towards the heart of the dome. What do you know? She had always been good at throwing. A better shot than the HUD's suggestion. Maybe the hull distorted things slightly ... and a flash. Not too bright, thanks to the helmet's anti-glare, but far bigger than the single explosions. Opal couldn't see anything for smoke.

"And?"

"It's destroyed. Vaporised. And something strange – it's cracked the hull."

"A small bang like that? Even passenger liners are built to withstand impacts from pirate attacks and space rocks."

"Agreed. The hull should be much thicker. But it isn't. At least in that spot. It's cracked a wide ravine, the hull's only thirty centimetres thick, and it leads straight into the interior compartments."

"It's a way in."

"It's sealing up."

"Shit."

"Somehow repairing itself. Faster than hardening gel or nanobots would."

"Time to seal?"

"At this rate – fifty-five seconds."

The HUD highlights showed that the remaining two turrets were now erupting from the masses of plastic-like tissue. They'd be targeting her any second. Opal seized the grapple gun, kept her foot lodged to prevent recoil, and took aim at the hole.

"Wait!" said Clarissa. "Aim beyond."

At any second Opal expected hammer bolts to pulverise her. No time for arguing or indecision. She aimed beyond the hole, fired, and the trailing cable straightened ahead of her as the head attached. She clicked retract at the same time as unhooking her foot, and once again flew over the hull as if she wore a rocket pack. A glance back showed huge gouges as bone bolts thunked into the ridge where she'd been. And then they stopped. They were reacquiring her.

"I'm going to miss it!" Opal said.

"Only partly true. The grapple is connected some distance beyond the hull crack, but I think it is important. I analysed the turret firing trajectories. They weren't shooting at you – they were targeting the *anchor point*. They worked out where you would stop. You were lucky to make it over the top with just a severed cable."

"So I let go before that point ..."

"Yes."

"Thanks."

The hole whizzed closer, still fringed in dark particles and fragments of tissue. She could see the crack as a jagged tear, fizzing at the edges. She had to let go of the grapple gun, push off it so she drifted down and through the impromptu gap. Timing. It always came down to that.

"Do you want a countdown?" Clarissa asked.

"No."

Opal licked her lips. Despite the ideal humidity in the suit her mouth was dry. Mistime this and she'd bounce off the hull at high speed. Or thud into that ominous fizzing at the edge of the self-repairing hole. If that stuff was rebuilding hull in seconds, what would it do to a small organic being in a suit?

Relax. Breathe deeply. She'd had near-escapes in combat before. Feel the adrenaline, don't be ruled by it. Reflexes ready to act. Eyes take in information, body judges. Instinct trumps reason.

Closer, a jagged black gash, though already its shape was softening and shrinking.

She twisted slightly, then pushed, relinquishing the grapple gun. Down towards the hull. Down towards the hole. And down towards the edges, with the acidic bubbling. Nothing to push against now, she'd mistimed, she was going to hit the edge ... then things shifted, jerked almost, and she was down, her perspective switching to an inner chamber, a room with chairs and a table, a dark meeting room. The table filled her vision as she smacked into it, scraped and tumbled and drifted up; she grabbed a chair's back in reflex, it must have been bolted to the ground, and she swung round until her feet landed heavily on the floor. Above her was a rapidly-shrinking view of space. The areas being sealed looked different from the rest of the ceiling – newer, untarnished, stretched, hardening toffee.

"I was going to miss ..."

"I activated the suit's jets. A microburst of air. You were close."

"But not close enough. Thanks."

The final bit of black sky disappeared as the hull closed.

"Question," said Clarissa. "I monitored you closely. Heart rate, pupil dilation and perspiration all matched data recordings of humans on rollercoasters. So does that mean it was fun?"

"No. Not fun. Fun's good excitement."

"I see. Thank you for the insight. Understanding what a thrill feels like is one of my difficulties. I'd like to experience a thrill one day."

"Stick around."

Opal unslung the recoilless rifle and edged along with her back to the smooth outer wall, targeting possible hiding places before she moved into their line of sight. Nothing.

"By the way, I was right," said Clarissa. "The guns pummelled the point you'd have reached. There would have been nothing left."

"Double thanks. But I'll miss that grapple gun."

At least she was in.

# CHASED

## ... 25 ...

The room was shadowy, a mysterious murk full of hiding places, but at least not pitch black due to a pale light from angled ceiling windows. They were cracked – possibly shock connected to the grenades – but held, and didn't seem in any danger of immediate blowout. Opal activated the helmet's silverlight. It radiated gentle fluorescence in each direction, and when combined with the visor's enhancement properties, it meant she could see clearly.

"So there's gravity," said Opal, as she climbed onto the long table for a better view. "The ship's engines must have power."

"Yes. Gravity is low – zero point four standard – but enough to keep you the right way up, especially with the suit's weight. Yet I cannot detect anything powering a magnetogravitic system."

"Atmosphere?"

"Voided on entry, but sealed now. Traces. Nothing new being vented in. We'll find out about the rest of the ship when we leave the room."

Opal moved down the table, scanning from side to side, sometimes facing back. The table's surface looked like it was thick with dust but she left no footprints. She knelt, scuffed a finger along the surface. It seemed to be rough.

"What's it made of?" she asked.

"Place your palm on the table."

Opal did as requested.

"Inconclusive," said Clarissa. "Some carbon, but also crystalline structures. It's all one material. The rough surface is part of it. Not wood, metal, alloy. For unknown reasons it doesn't scan properly."

"So we have a table that looks like a normal dust-covered table, but isn't. Notice anything else?" Opal scanned up the length of the table. She'd walked partway along it, but it extended much further, over fifty metres. There were hundreds of chairs neatly placed at the sides.

"Please elucidate."

"Who ever heard of a table this long? I mean, this doesn't look like a canteen. It's more like a meeting room. See, there's even a wall screen, but it's way longer than any I've ever seen."

"It certainly doesn't match standard designs."

"Like it's all stretched. No, the chairs are to scale. Like something built from a description when you don't understand the function. Do you feel this? The weirdness?"

"I do not feel anything but agree that this is not what I would expect."

Opal reached the end of the table and vaulted down in silence. Meeting rooms. Chatter and gestures and secret power struggles. Life. But there was none of it here.

As she approached the door she expected it to slide open for her. Even on this strange ship, expectations die hard. But it did not move. Broken detector, or power issues? There was no obvious manual release. She crouched and slipped the fingers of her left hand into the groove at the bottom, then stood. If there was resistance the suit's strength hid it. When the door first moved she heard a high-pitched whistle, then a deeper whooshing sound as gases were sucked into the room to fill the void. The door slid up high enough for her to step under. When Opal tapped her fingers against the wall she heard the patter. It was as if her ears had been cleared.

"So there is an atmosphere," she told Clarissa.

"Yes. Not standard ship air though. It's a strange mix. Some nitrogen and oxygen, but also xenon, argon, fluorine, trace exotics. I'm not aware of anything that would breathe this. Conceivably the atmospro is malfunctioning, or it is remnants from an accident. No detectable bacteria or viruses in the air, but there are mould spores."

"Are those the green specks swirling around?"

"Yes. I don't recognise their provenance."

Opal stepped into a corridor. Her lights gave a clear view for a short distance before fading into shadow. The air seemed thick, with an overall greenish tinge. It was like being under water. She held a palm out, and a few specks settled on it. The visor enhanced and magnified them, but they still just looked like tiny lumps, green microtumours. She wiped her palm.

"I want to get to the bridge. That'll give the best chance of finding out what ship this is, where it's been, right?" And maybe what happened to the crew and passengers.

"Yes. I have plans for various vessels in memory. For now I can just point you in the general direction based on my external view, but if the patterns match any of my plans I can then give more accurate directions. Based on the observation tower and meeting room I would suggest you are in the privileged and corporate sections."

A ghostly arrow appeared in the view, so Opal moved carefully down the narrow corridor in that direction, weapon lowered but ready. At junctions she swung round the corner, rifle raised, targeting any shapes. But it was always closed doorways, domed passages, panelled walls and green dust.

"No signage at intersections," she noted. "Directions, info-screens, whatever. Just some kind of score marks." Opal ran a hand over them. Elongated indentations at different heights.

"That is peculiar."

She continued to go straight, aware of her breathing, trying to keep it calm. The silence made her feel claustrophobic. Strange, that wasn't normally a weakness of hers. Maybe it was another feeling beneath it all, of being watched, but she hadn't noticed any cameras. Each time she glanced back she saw nothing but shadow. And that made her suspicious of the shadows. The blackness.

She temporarily boosted the lights to increase the range, and the black retreated, revealing ... more of the same.

Jumpy. Just jumpy. And yet the longer she headed down this disused passage, the more vulnerable she felt.

At the next door she halted. She had to bend and raise the door manually again. It was a dangerous moment of exposure. She was tense, ready to step back and fire a warning shot if anything threatening crouched on the other side.

An office. Shelves with no books. A picture frame but the picture was obscured by sparkling dust. A wide desk of fake wood. A terminal on it. A small vent at the top of a wall. She gave a last glance up and down the corridor and entered the room, moved around the desk quickly so she faced the door again. Of course, having that restricted view out was almost worse – it was too easy to imagine something silently moving up the corridor and crouching outside her exit.

"You would tell me if you detected anything, right?" Opal asked. "You're always scanning?"

"Of course. Suit sensors inside, Hedgehogs and ship outside. I would alert you."

"Right."

"It is understandable to feel jumpy on boarding a potentially hostile ship."

"I know. It feels somehow more than that but ... never mind."

Opal swept the desk in front of the terminal clean of the green sediment-like dust then touched the screen. Nothing. She waved her hand in front of it. "No holographic controls or keyboard," she observed. She swiped her hand once more without expectation, but this time a control panel did appear in front of the screen, projected from its base, and the display glowed with cold blue phosphorescence.

"Delayed?" she asked.

Clarissa didn't answer. Maybe she assumed it was a statement.

Opal worked the controls, but nothing more happened. No system menus, no proper interface. Just the semblance of one – a flat glowing screen.

"The lights are on but nobody's home. Can you interface directly?" she asked.

"Not with a client terminal. Too dumb."

"Figures."

There was nothing else in here. Back to the corridor then. She raised the rifle and moved towards the doorway. Stay low, one way then the other from within the room before stepping out. It will be clear, she told herself. Nothing there. Nothing waiting. She licked her dry lips. Only stepping out –

"Wait," said Clarissa.

Opal froze, weapon levelled at the doorway.

"Not out there. On the wall by the shelves."

Opal looked round – there. A pinkish patch. Like a growth of flesh-coloured mildew. She stepped closer.

"Don't touch it," Clarissa warned. "It wasn't there when we came in."

"You sure? I could have missed it, it's small."

"I compared it to the recording. It began to form while you were at the terminal."

"And it's just out of sight of where I stood ..."

"Yes."

It seemed to bubble, grow, chewing gum expansions.

"I think you should leave," said Clarissa.

"I agree."

Opal backed away towards the doorway. Didn't want to stay in this room any longer. She lunged through and across the corridor, low, hitting the far wall where she crouched and faced both ways, then back at the room. Nothing in the corridor, but there was a noise from the room she'd left, a subdued popping sound. Innocuous, non-threatening. She started running.

"Let's hope this is the right way," said Opal, as she raced down the corridor. At a junction she scanned each way, rifle raised, then ran on in the direction of the arrow's insistent flashing. This ribbed passage sloped downwards, tightening like a throat. More picture frames lined it, the images obscured by green dust.

"Movement," warned Clarissa. "From behind."

"How many?" Opal risked a glance backward but saw only shadow.

"Multiple targets of human-like mass. Moving erratically but closing."

Opal ran faster, the suit enhancing her actions so she covered ground with huge strides, helped by the low gravity.

"Ahead too," said Clarissa. "Closing from the side passages of the next corridor. If you go faster you'll cross the junction before they reach it."

"I need to get somewhere with more space. This is a rat run."

"I'm doing my best. Currently trying to locate the central pedestrian hub."

Even with the suit's aid, running full sprint was tiring. She couldn't keep it up forever. She reached the first junction and gritted her teeth, sensing or imagining ominous motion close by, expecting to be grabbed, avoiding looking down the dark passages to left and right, only focussing on where she was going. Then she was through, unscathed.

"Next junction, turn right. They're coming from ahead and the left," Clarissa said.

"It feels like they're funnelling me."

"Not enough data to support that."

At the junction Opal stopped, knelt, raised the rifle and aimed down the left corridor. The thick murky greenness still swirled in her wake. It was like being at the bottom of the sea.

"Range?"

"Three hundred metres."

"Can you enhance?"

The visor's view cycled through different colour schemes, eventually locking on one that showed elongated forms apparently moving through the air from wall to wall as they approached. Not bipedal.

"Infrared was no good, they're the same temperature as the ship, but there's electrical potential so I focussed on that."

Opal targeted the nearest as it zigged across the hall, a computer-generated blob rather than whatever reality was closing in through the green murk.

"Optimal firing range," said Clarissa.

Opal's finger depressed the trigger but held. "I can't assume it's a threat," she said. "It could be a new lifeform. Something to communicate with."

"Two hundred and fifty metres. Similar distance to your right. Also coming from the route you took, even closer. More than twenty targets."

"Shit."

Opal held her aim, tracking the lead. It was almost within visible range, when the atmosphere would be thinner, the light brighter, and she'd see it unaided.

"Send out messages," Opal said. "Every known language, every frequency."

"What should I say?"

"Hello, for starters! Peace and love and hippy shit to follow. Now, blast it!"

Clarissa began transmitting, some of it in Opal's voice.

They were still coming, shapes looming from the murk.

"Three vectors all congregating on you, fast," Clarissa announced in the helmet while messages continued to be broadcast outside. "You have to fire or move."

Opal cursed, let go of the trigger and started running down the safe route.

"Keep transmitting, every variant you can think of."

"It will make it easier for them to track you."

"I don't think they were having trouble before."

Words and sounds continued to echo down the corridors from the suit's loudspeakers, cycling through things she understood, things she vaguely recognised (was that Longping Code?), and things that sounded like whale noises.

"I think one of those other passages would have led to a social atrium," Clarissa told her.

"Big space?"

"Yes."

"Definitely funnelling me away then. Any other route to –"

Suddenly Opal stumbled, an impact on the back of her knee had collapsed her leg, sending her clattering to the floor. She scrambled up, noting projectiles thumping into the walls nearby. She continued running, hunched forward to make a smaller target.

"They're firing at me."

"The bullets resemble bone shards." Clarissa enlarged a freeze-framed image to the side of the display. "High velocity and serrated. The suit retains integrity."

Another pinged off Opal's shoulder, spinning her so she glanced off the wall, but she didn't lose momentum, didn't look back.

"So much for peace," she panted, taking the first turning to get out of the line of fire. Her knee throbbed.

"It may be an alien attempt at communication."

"Seems all-too-human to me." Wall blurred past. The corridor was widening. That meant something. "Keep broadcasting, just in case."

"You're coming to a three-way junction. Go left."

Opal took the turning at a sharp angle, using one leg to kick off the corner wall and keep up her momentum. The corridor curved.

"They're closing," Clarissa stated.

Opal just sprinted on, trying to keep her breathing regular, one arm holding the rifle against her chest.

She rounded the bend. Ahead was a ceiling-height glass door showing a huge room beyond – some kind of mezzanine with benches, staircases, decorative-but-unlit globes dangling from cables up above.

The door didn't open.

Opal kicked the glass hard, rebounding off without shattering it. She tried a punch from her left fist, using all the suit's muscle. Again, an echoing crash but no way through.

"Emergency material, diamond-structured, super strong," Clarissa warned. "Motion closing from behind."

Opal swung round, knelt in a firing stance, rifle raised. "Suggestions?" Particles swirled around her, disturbed by her movements. She suppressed the sensation of drowning. Focus.

"I've modified one of the grenades to be a directional charge," Clarissa told her. "It's ready, once placed it will detonate a few seconds later."

Opal reached across her body with her left hand, removed the small round disc. One side of it was sticky. She slapped it on the glass behind her without looking and aimed again. The first of her pursuers rounded the corner into her sights.

It was over a metre long, with a heavy look to the streamlined but flattened grey torso. Something like a squashed and distorted dolphin, perhaps the flaps of skin resembling fins. Spiny protrusions swept behind it, but it was the front that drew her attention – an extended blade-like twist of gristle with bony tooth-like serrations edging it like a saw, sprouting from what might be a stunted head. The blade swung left to right, swiping the air ahead of it like a sword. The creature itself seemed to drift, fast, from one wall to another as it approached.

"With regret, I suggest you fire," said Clarissa. "Your safety overrides all other considerations."

Opal grimaced. Advice from a mind with short-circuited ethical constraints didn't help.

She could start shooting.

They might be protecting their home. They might have babies. Parents. Sisters.

Another creature was visible beyond the first, a pod of them looming just further.

Sleek like dolphins, maybe intelligent like dolphins.

They were almost upon her.

Her bullets could shatter minds and bodies.

But they, also, had some way of firing organic projectiles. Block line of sight.

She shifted directly in front of the first creature, feeling relief that it was now too late to shoot, a decision made for her.

She raised her rifle to parry the bony blade. Only then did Opal notice that where the creature skimmed off the wall it seemed to leave etched scuffs, like deep acid burns. Fuck.

A thwump from behind. The explosive.

She blocked and shifted to the side at the last second, just enough to avoid the brunt of the impact but the creature's momentum sent both of them crashing backwards into the glass door. The charge must have worked – they ploughed through and thick crystal exploded around them in dagger-like shards.

When she hit the ground on her back she rolled awkwardly in the crunching glass, got up running, sprinted across the open space of the massive atrium.

Red warning signs on the HUD, acid damage.

She peeked over her shoulder – one of the creatures seemed to contract so the trailing spines twisted forward, glistening bone shards began to ping off her suit, she only just kept her balance as more of the things skimmed through the broken doorway. The repulsor shields could deflect glancing blows, but not direct hits.

No more time for niceties, only reaction.

She knelt and fired, grouping her shots. The creature bucked and spun, avoiding at least one of the bullets. Lightning reactions. Greyish liquid in the air, clouding and removing visibility. No noises, no screams. Shot after shot into the mass, but it only seemed to slow them.

"The bullets are passing through," Clarissa told her. "Seem to be damaging them, but not fatally. Possibly no critical internal organs. I suggest you run."

Opal didn't need telling twice.

She fired blindly backwards with one hand as she took a long seat at a jump, skimming over the top. More obstacles in the way, sediment-covered furniture, long unused, a ghost chamber. Always quicker to go over than round. The weapon clicked empty. She skidded across an ornate table, ejecting the spent magazine and clipping a new one in place before her feet touched the ground on the other side. A second to look back – more of the beings pouring from the broken doorway, hardly visible now the murk thickened with distance, but still coming, skimming up off the floor in arcs and back down, some sliding under furniture towards her, some wounded but unslowed. She looked for options as she ran. The open atrium was a danger, they were spreading out, would flank her. She headed for a long staircase upwards. An escalator, but dead like everything else, the metal steps locked into position, she bounded up three at a time. The atrium ceiling was so high she could only just make out the huge skywindows that would have provided an amazing view out to space if the atmosphere hadn't been clogged with green murk.

"Suggestions?" she shouted.

"Bullets ineffective. I'll drop some of the remaining grenades, different payloads, observe the results. You keep running."

"Good plan. And you can quit broadcasting hellos."

The loudspeakers silenced, leaving only her breath and clanging footsteps on the metal stairs, and faint hissing sounds from below.

Opal reached the top. Explosions behind her. Presumably the suit was able to also eject the grenades like mines. She looked back to see thick black smoke, and another flash from within. A grey body flung horizontally, spreading whitish fluids. A glimpse of the underside showed a pulsing soft tissue that reminded Opal of jellyfish. Another creature moving slowly, lost or injured. Gruesome scenes, whatever the species.

More of the things emerged from the smoke cloud apparently dazed, but seeming to detect her and drift-sliding towards the escalator. Opal shouldered the rifle and ran through some kind of commercial section. Glass-fronted display cases lined the walls to each side.

"Preliminary findings," Clarissa said. "The beings are unaffected by smoke and light. Explosives caused some damage. Shall I blow them apart?"

"Last resort. Any other options?"

"Strong disorientation effects from electrical phenomenon, suggestive of an organism with a nervous system. Although the snouts may double as weapons, enhancement of still images shows they are fimbriated with tiny pores. I think they are electrical detectors – similar systems in other species are used for navigation and prey-location, generating an electrical map of the local area."

"Conveniently well-suited to this environment, especially with the power turned off. Okay, enough hurt for now. No more explosives. Drop EMPs and I'll try to escape while they're confused."

"Very well. If they also have pack-behaviour then enough of a threat may deter them, at least temporarily. But I only have a few grenades left, and your safety is –"

"Just do it."

Opal stayed on the commercial route until Clarissa had launched the grenades, primed for proximity. Despite the suit's shielding the HUD flickered with each blast but regained full imagery quickly. Opal's respect for the systems keeping her alive just kept growing. She drew the energy pistol as she ran and switched it to EMP.

"How we doing?" she asked.

"Pursuit slowing. Seems to have stunned a number of them. A few are still coming though."

A point reinforced by one of the shop windows to Opal's right exploding inwards, shattered by whizzing bone bolts.

Opal aimed backwards and fired a few shots as she ran. Each blast had a radius of effect so she didn't have to be too accurate anyway; one of the beings thudded against a wall and smacked down heavily, writhing spastically and revealing more of the raw underneaths that seemed to hide toothy organs or attachments Opal didn't want to contemplate.

Another shop window boomed into shrapnel beside her, debris raining to the floor. She decided it was time to get off the straights anyway – they were faster in that direction. She veered into the storefront, ploughing into human-type shop dummies modelling outfits and sending them flying, her arms crossed in front of her face as she crunched over glassy fragments and stumbled when a billowy dress got wrapped around her head and blocked her vision. She snatched it off and brushed away broken limbs – shit, shop mannequins were creepy things – then scrambled over the counter, knocking parcels to the side. There was a door to the rear, but no time to open it. She leaned over the counter and aimed her pistol at the shattered shop entrance.

Even in here, an apparently sealed area, the air swirled with the algae-like greenness, the shawls and capes fluttered in low gravity as if drifting in water.

As soon as one of the creatures slid across the sill she opened fire; she missed but the pulsing flash was maybe enough, because the being darted jerkily back into the gloom.

She aimed again. Green motes eddied. Her hand shook slightly. She took deep breaths. Nothing else came.

"I can scan a small distance through the walls," Clarissa said. "They are retreating. At various speeds. Or at least looking to come at you from a different direction."

"That's good enough for me."

Opal checked the pistol's charge. Still half left. She holstered it, raised and slipped under the doorway, then pulled it down behind her. Hopefully she was safe from pursuit.

This was a storage room with another door at the back. Naked mannequins held out arms, beseeching.

"No bodies so far. Crew or passengers. Weird," she said.

"I am scanning for signs of life at all times, but nothing."

"Maybe holed up somewhere. Or evacuated. Captured and removed by pirates? Eaten? My hopes of finding them alive are shrinking."

"Is that why you are on board? A rescue mission?"

Opal ignored the question and swept dust from boxes. Tore one open. Clothes. No – material. Stitched but strangely shaped. Certainly not outfits for sale. She held one up.

"Like props," she said. "Not meant to be examined too closely. Reminds me of the terminal, and the long table." Opal glanced again at the plastic figures around her. "Tell me something. You're observing all the time. It's not possible those things out there were weird illusions? Somehow I've been shooting at crew, thinking they were a threat?"

"No. The acid-resistance of the suit prevented breach from your contact, and the bone shards didn't penetrate either. The suit is sealed, so you are free of biological influence, and hallucinogenics wouldn't affect me."

Opal breathed a sigh of relief.

"At least, it is a very low probability that you were killing sentients of your own species," Clarissa added.

"It's so reassuring having an AI to chat to."

Opal opened the rear door. None of them locked, just powered down.

"A question," said Clarissa. "Why are you here? You have been cryptic so far."

Opal sighed. "I suppose you've earned something. Look, Lost Ships are supposed to pay out in some way."

"If you make it back in one piece."

"Yes. If I survive."

"Partial records suggest you have been researching this for a long time. Most of your adult life. It must be such a tiring quest."

"You could say that. Following rumours that are mostly false. Clues that go to dead ends."

"So you are hoping to get rich or powerful?"

"Not quite. Let's just say it's my only chance of a new life. Leave it at that for now."

No reply. Maybe Clarissa was satisfied with the answer; maybe she took Opal's last sentence literally.

Opal stepped into a narrow service walkway. Didn't bother with a firearm, Clarissa seemed to be pretty reliable as an early warning system. The HUD's directional arrow pointed left. She went left.

# DISTURBED

## ... 24 ...

She stuck to the small service corridors for a while, sometimes having to squeeze through gaps between unmarked storage
crates that seemed to have been abandoned there during trans-
portation. Then she cut through staff administration areas –
work cubicles, observation posts, planning rooms. No bodies,
no alien species, not even much in the way of objects and furniture. It was too tidy, too empty, didn't feel like there'd been a
disaster: didn't feel like it had ever been lived in. She tried a few
of the terminals. Again, she got control panels but no interactive
display. If she wanted answers, the bridge and central systems
were the only likely place. Still on Plan A. And she was getting
closer.

Opal drank as she walked. A straw extended inside the helmet
so she could sip nutrient-rich water. She didn't care about the
nutritional value, she was just pleased that it was chilled and
refreshing. The straw retracted when she'd had enough.

She took a service ladder up two floors, quicker than using the public footways. She came out of the top hatch with her rifle ready. Shadows shifted every time her head moved and swept the silverlight beam across cramped passages with bulky struts that created too many hiding places. Again she felt like she was being watched. She passed through the area as quickly as she could, wary of each dark alcove. She was glad to leave that section and pull the door down behind her. She watched it for a minute while resting, but it didn't move. Nothing followed. Just imagination doing its job too well.

An open doorway led her to kitchens. Industrial food processors were built along two of the walls, conveyors in front. But there were also real thermal plates and pans. Real cooking. It seemed out of place to come across that, but she remembered the luxury status of this kind of ship. Many passengers would pay a premium for "real" food, the old slow way, rather than reconstituted proteins and nutrients formed and heated to resemble hand-made meals. She lifted the lid off a large pan. Inside was a gloopy liquid. It sloshed when she rattled the container. A stirring implement lay on the counter, so she used it to swirl the liquid round. Pieces of unrecognisable vegetable surfaced. She replaced the lid.

"Don't you think that's strange?" she asked Clarissa as she moved to the next bank of hot plates.

"I agree. It is not efficient."

"No. The preservation. Shouldn't it be mouldy?"

"True. Even if the lid was hermetically sealed there would be organisms that could multiply."

"And it's one of the first organic things we've come across. I think we should analyse it."

Another pan sat nearby. Opal removed its lid – and found a fur-covered mess of grey and black mould half-filled the pan. She replaced the lid quickly, even though the suit was sealed. There was something unpleasant about decay.

"That is what you originally expected," Clarissa said.

Opal frowned. The exit from the kitchens was ahead. Instead she returned to the first pan, the large one. Not even sure why, she took the lid off again.

Half the liquid was gone. Rafts of spidery mould hairs floated, sprouting black orbs.

"Perhaps when you first lifted the lid you let in a contaminant," said Clarissa.

"Perhaps."

The mould grew even as she watched.

"Do you still want to sample it?" Clarissa asked. "You could insert your palm."

"I'm not putting my hand in that." The spores were nearing the top of the pot. Opal slammed the lid down. "I'm pretty sure it wouldn't analyse as standard food constituents. Like everything else on this ship. Just a little bit off." She backed away from the pot but also glanced around. No visible cameras. And her words couldn't be heard outside the suit anyway. Lip-reading?

"Is there anybody listening in?" Opal mouthed soundlessly.

No answer from outside, but Opal had forgotten that Clarissa was monitoring her every action: "The suit is sealed, so –"

"No, that wasn't aimed at you," Opal interrupted, taking a second to stretch some of the tension out of her arms. "Hey, Clarissa, put me on loudspeaker."

"Done."

Opal repeated her question to the room then waited, scanning around for any movements.

Nothing. Apart from the pan lid, which seemed to be lifting.

Okay, time to go. She shut off the loudspeaker. When Clarissa questioned her about what she was doing Opal just replied that it was a hunch. That seemed like a more positive spin than admitting to paranoia.

Out of the kitchens, lifting and slamming down the door again.

She was on a tiled walkway suspended above another atrium. On her right were entrances to various catering and staff rooms, and occasionally the open alcoves of social juice and alcohol bars, now looking decidedly unsocial with their coverings of green dust over the high stools and artificial plants. On her left a railing protected her from a huge drop to the floor far below. Up here she was nearer to the skywindows, which appeared as huge black oblongs, the interior atmosphere too thick to show details such as starfield backdrops.

This atrium was a vast catering hall. Tables of different sizes spread across the ground, some of them obviously for VIP guests – the smaller ones, the more private ones, those on higher platforms with views across all the lower-status tables. She could imagine how loud it would have been up here when the hall below was full. All that chatter and life and laughter booming up. And now ... she remembered a documentary she'd seen once about recovering sunken boats from the seabeds of oceanic planets, like the one she'd lived on for a while. The way the air deepened in murky green as she looked down brought the alien environments of deep-sea waters back to mind. Lonely graves, slowly decaying. To be stuck here, in dead silence, so far from home. You would drift. Bodies floating about you. Weightless. Resemblance of what they used to be, but empty shells. At-tractors for predators. You hide in fear amongst the rust and sediment. Needing to have contact. Needing something. Black-ness above. No way up to the escape. No way to get free alone. Praying for a lifeline. A light. Won't someone lower a light to you? A glow of hope, warmth you could squeeze into, food that wasn't decayed. Praying for something to sate the hunger, the cold, the loneliness –

"Opal!" Clarissa said, loud and abrupt.

Opal pushed back off the railing, dizzy. She had been leaning over precariously.

"What is it?" She bit her lip to snap out of the dream-like feeling.

"You weren't responding. I had to administer a stimulant."

"How long?"

"Forty-three seconds."

"How could that happen?" Opal was walking briskly now, avoiding looking down to the floor below. "There isn't a leak in the suit, is there?"

"No. All sealed. But I did detect something down there. Your gaze never locked onto it but ... something was moving along under the tables. Getting closer to the point below you. You had just started to lean over the railing when I gave up on calling your name and took more drastic action."

Opal shuddered. "Let's hope it can't climb." Those words didn't make her feel any more secure so she broke into a run. "And thanks again. This ship is full of surprises. Any ideas on distance to the bridge?"

"Based on the layouts I think we're getting close. We are in the upper third of the ship, and now towards the fore. Far down below would be the main passenger quarters, and we have avoided all that area."

"Finally the girl gets a break."

Opal kept her distance from the railing and was glad when a side-route led her away from the dining area.

"Opal, I have another question. It was inspired by your metaphor of breaking into a house through an open window earlier."

"Okaaaay," Opal said, cautiously.

"Personnel files show you have a criminal record. For breaking in to government and corporate databases. Since enforcement is rarely perfect, probabilities suggest the record is incomplete and you did it other times without being caught."

"Just as well. There are systems that spell death if you're trapped with your fingers in them."

"What I have been thinking about is the hacking."

Shit. "I order you to forget that line of inquiry."

"What line?" asked Clarissa.

Humour or honesty or subterfuge? Sometimes it felt like Opal had made a deal with the devil.

Opal was passing through a crew-only maintenance section, where cleaning and transport machinery seemed locked in place but provided comforting cover as she made her way across to a bank of elevators. She wasn't hopeful as she passed their doors, but suddenly there was a hum. She spun, rifle raised – one of the elevators' doors had opened. Dim artificial light flickered inside.

Opal backed away, moving in a semicircle to try and view the interior of the chamber. It seemed to be empty. Then she cursed herself for being preoccupied and whirled to view back the way she had come, in case it was a distraction. Forklifts, inert repairbots, storage canisters: no visible predators.

"So there's power now?" Opal asked.

"I'm not detecting any."

"Why did this door open, but not the others?"

"Conceivably there are problems in some areas, but not others."

"Which might mean something special about this place. Where does that lift go?"

"Towards ... the bridge."

"So we get close to the bridge and things start working." Opal's rifle shifted from shadow to shadow: target, confirm, move on. "That's a bit of a coincidence, wouldn't you say?"

"Perhaps there is something at the bridge with limited range. Only now can they monitor us."

"That doesn't reassure me."

The lift stood open. Inviting. The stylishly curved doors like a smiling mouth. A shortcut. So convenient.

Opal sighed, ignored the elevator, and moved on quickly. Never stay still. Never make yourself a target. She began to climb a twisting staircase. This was the hard way. But she hated the feeling of being herded. Since she'd left the army she'd set one main rule: her life would be on her own terms.

As she rounded the first bend in the stairs she heard a hum as the elevator doors closed. Probably just a proximity detector giving up. And yet her gut insisted she was being watched, more than ever. She hoped the long route was the right choice.

Opal kept the rifle raised, covering each small landing up above as she ascended, and every so often looking down at where she'd come from. She moved at a swift pace. Staircases were a danger. Only two directions. Ambushes were easy to set up if an aggressor was given time. So don't give them time.

It was easier in the low gravity, and with the suit's movement enhancers. A few clanging bounds and she'd be on the next half-level, a good view both ways through the dusty motes that floated across her vision. Echoes faded to silence before she moved on.

She rounded the corner on her eleventh ascension and spotted something dark just as the HUD highlighted it. She aimed the weapon and was ready to fire. Mass showed as greater than human. It didn't move.

"Biological. Apparently inert," Clarissa said.

Opal edged closer, placing her feet carefully on each stair. A roundish mass of tumorous crimson tissue that seemed to grow from the wall. The surface was blackened and ash-like, flaking.

"It resembles those pink growths we saw earlier," Clarissa said.

"But a hell of a lot larger."

"Yes. Maybe they expand over time."

"Ideas?"

"Some kind of fast-growing being? Fleshy, but behaving like mould or fungus?"

"Then what's this?" Opal aimed her headset light at something that stuck out from the centre. An emaciated, stick-like protrusion that disappeared into a layered crusted split. "Looks like a human arm."

"Yes."

"Something pulled into it ... or coming out."

"Yes."

"But it isn't pink and bubbling. Looks like it's been flamed. Another being on the ship did this."

"Possible, but one must not jump to conclusions in a place like this. It could be part of a lifecycle."

"Hmm."

"I just wanted to inform you that I've detected exterior movement."

"Another ship?"

"No. Nothing to worry about: seems to be a standard rocky mass moving at fairly high velocity. No doubt it will be captured by the gravity well and fall in eventually. I'm just informing you for completeness."

"Thanks. If anything changes let me know."

As Opal ascended she saw more of the sickening burnt and twisted growths lining the stairs. Scorch marks on the walls around them sometimes. And something else. A low vibration. She felt it in her ears, in her spine, a rough sandpaper pressure, yet Clarissa claimed to detect nothing.

It was good to leave the charnel house of the staircase. As she entered a wide corridor finished in the smart panelled decor of command, the vibration seemed even stronger. She was getting closer to the source, but the funereal silence seemed oppressive. "I think there are different forces on this ship," she said, just to make conversation, to hear words. "Not necessarily unified."

"Conjecture," replied Clarissa.

"Something at the bridge wants me to come this way."

No response. Opal looked through windows to offices as she moved along, sometimes wiping the green residue off the polymer glass first for a better view. No bodies.

"Maybe whatever is on the bridge destroyed the growths. For whatever reason. Might have been like one force fighting another. Or a host destroying a parasite."

"Interesting theories, Opal."

The vibration wasn't physical, but it pulled. Like gravity, a force drawing her on. Implacable. Yearning. She shook her head to clear it.

Following Clarissa's directions, which were getting surer now, they crossed an open-plan control room split across different levels. At first Opal thought she'd reached the bridge but Clarissa said there was a bit more ascending to do.

All the empty monitoring stations, dust on seats, particles in the air, forever watching dead display screens. One large screen overlooked the area, but it too was blank, and it had been cracked at some point by a tremendous force. Despite the emptiness there was an undercurrent: the place emanated power, even in vestiges of death. And the force pulled even more, her neck hairs rising as if in an electrical charge. Opal's eyes were drawn to the correct exit, a short tunnel leading to a ladder upwards. It held her gaze like an eye would. She was wanted. Answers would be offered to her. And then she could leave.

"Observation: external temperature is cooler here. It has been dropping slightly as we've neared the bridge. One point seven degrees colder than the lower decks, and the rate is increasing. It will have no negative effect on you or the suit, but – alert! Oh no, they didn't –"

It was a shock to hear what sounded like frustration and panic in Clarissa's voice. Even with the human cadences there was usually a dryness to the voice – but for the first time it sounded as frightened as the real Clarissa would have.

Opal squatted and slammed her back against a control panel, looking every way for a threat, weapon ready.

"What is it? Where?"

"I'm sorry, Opal, I failed." Clarissa sounded tearful. So bizarre. "The threat isn't internal, you're in no immediate danger; it's outside. They weren't asteroids, they were military, cloaked. I've no record of systems that effective – none of the usual signatures of known devices."

"Shit! No chance they've missed us, or are here for something else?"

"No. Their course was imitating asteroids but has changed now that it's done its job of getting them close. And the cloaking was too perfect. They've only disabled it because I would have spotted the anomalies and detected them soon anyway. I can't decode the chatter – though I'll try, I might be able to crack it – but they know."

"ETA?"

"About fifteen minutes. Worse news: there are two ships. Hammer-class corvettes, fully armed, probably each with a complement of marines. They must really want us."

"No surprise there. Any chance of an evac for me? Could we outrun them?"

"By the time I collected you they'd be on us. They outgun me, probably outrun me too with their torsion drives."

"Okay. Get out of here, Clarissa. Head into the deep cloud, as far as you can without getting sucked down the gravity well."

"But the neutron star has an incredibly strong magnetic field – disruptive to my systems, like a permanent EMP if I got too close. I would rapidly lose communications with you!"

"I know. Direct orders. Hopefully they'll give chase. And you must stay out of contact of the mil-ships. No open ports, do not accept received messages, block all pings."

"Why?"

"Just do it!"

"Accelerating now."

"Obviously if you come up with a way to cripple or destroy them then do so, and come back for me later. Also: are there any parts of this vessel that would shield me from external communications? I'm talking total blackout." Time for Plan B. At least she'd prepared for this.

"The engine core, possibly," said Clarissa. "If you were right within the central systems. That has to be fully shielded to prevent interference, hacking, or field calibration errors."

"Highlight the location, I'm moving."

"Done."

"Anywhere near the bridge?"

"No. Opposite end of the ship. Quite a trek."

"Shit again."

Opal was running across the control room, one last glance at the bridge entrance – not enough time to get up there and do what needed doing. So fucking close! But if this fell apart now it had been pointless. She had to survive to make it worthwhile. Answers could wait.

"Why would you do this? Go to a shielded area?" Clarissa asked. "They already know we're here. Even if I shake off the corvettes and return I won't be able to communicate with you – won't be able to help or rescue you! I don't like this."

Clarissa wouldn't like the answer either, if Opal had time to explain. Just as well. Plan B was shaky enough already.

"No questions. Time's short. Tell me what to expect." Opal glanced at the range on the HUD as she left the control room, sprinting down open corridor, glad of the lack of people for once. No obstacles. "And how the heck am I going to cover the distance in time?"

"There's only one way. This kind of passenger liner always has a transit network running from the crew control sections. In fact, there are likely others throughout the ship but this is the most direct. The train tunnels are often referred to as the Spine, and use bullet cars that can traverse the ship in zero-g vacuum tunnels, over three hundred kilometres an hour."

"But don't they need power?"

"Yes. And we have none. With time I could rig something but there *is* no time. Maybe if you can get into a car there will be a hatch, use that to get into the tunnel. At least from there it's a straight line to the engine core. Part of the emergency response procedures: command and control are the two priority components."

Opal shouldered the rifle. It just slowed her down. Typically some of the doors were closed, and had to be manually raised. If the military got close enough to Clarissa ... not worth thinking about. She'd done all she could. Now was time to respond and move, not to worry. She checked the time display on the HUD, then began a countdown in her head.

# DISABLED

## ... 23 ...

As she ran she was again aware of the lack of signage. A ship like this should have smart signs everywhere that ran without power and indicated key destinations. Transport, recreation, emergency routes, observation decks. Apart from burns and scratches, the walls were mostly featureless. She focussed on the flashing directional arrow in the HUD. It was her lifeline in this place. Hopefully it would still work even when Clarissa was out of range.

Ceiling lights began to flicker on and off, brightening the atmosphere to pea soup before dropping back to shadow. It was the first time she'd seen them active. And she knew it wasn't some automated detector, because she felt the bridge's pull weakening, like cold elastic being stretched. Something was trying to communicate with her, halt her, bring her back. Fascinating. But it would have to be later. She ran on with no idea what was in the rooms around her. Only the curving corridor mattered.

"Clarissa?"

After a second's delay: "Yes."

"While you're out of commspace see if you can work out how they tracked us. Since we switched trajectories so many times to throw pursuit there must be something else. We'll never get away if we overlooked a bug or compromised system that's calling out without your knowledge. Find it and fry it."

"I will ... try."

"How long before we lose contact completely?"

Another delay. "Minutes."

Okay. Comms fading but working slowly. No doubt there'd be distortion soon.

The corridor lights had gone out completely, walls only illuminated by the suit's helmet again. Maybe whatever was at the bridge was out of range now.

"Opal ... update. Only one of the ... ships is following me ... gaining. The other ... changed course. For the Lost Ship. Lining up for docking."

Oh boy. She was going to have company. Highly trained and equipped ruthless company.

She could imagine their commander's amazement. They reached their target of a stolen ship and escaped renegade soldier only to find the trail had also led them to a treasure they didn't know existed, and they'd caught Opal red-handed digging it out of the sand. Their lucky day. She bet they could taste the promotions. She cursed herself for leading them here.

Movement ahead. She was about to draw her weapon when she recognised it.

An open bulkhead further down the corridor. A super-strong internal door that could close off sections in emergencies, whether decompression or pirate boardings. There was no manual way of raising one of those once it locked into place.

And it started to lower, with a deep wheeze of long-unused machinery. Maybe the bridge didn't give up easily. But was it trying to protect her, or trap her? Same outcome either way.

Opal was tired but sprinted faster, giving it all she had so the suit recognised the need and added its own power. Walls and floor blurred as she focussed on the descending door.

"Opal ..."

Some crackling in the voice. She ignored it, leaning forwards and propelling herself at an angle that wouldn't have been possible in standard gravity. The soles of the suit had fantastic grip.

Halfway down. She could see the thickness of the door in the silvery light from her helmet. The long sprint was exhausting but she had to make it. Keep her breathing regular, fast but in rhythm with her movements.

Another option popped into her mind – maybe the bridge was protecting itself from the next group of intruders? Whatever the motivation, she still had to get through.

The door was down to half a metre from the groove that would secure it forever. She dived, twisted and rolled on her side, momentum from the suit's speed carrying her forward as she tumbled and skidded to a halt just beyond the door. It thwumped down heavily next to her, shaking the ground. She'd never been so pleased to be staring up at a ceiling. Her chest heaved too much to laugh.

"Opal ... something's wrong ..."

Opal scrambled up despite wanting to just close her eyes and go to sleep. She gave the blast door a kick then started jogging away from it. The range finder blinked. Three hundred metres and closing. Almost at the transport car.

"I'm listening."

"I'm turning down ... attempts to signal from the military ... but my systems ... there's a divergence."

"Plain English."

"Something's spreading in ... to my consciousness. Data packets. No known source."

Already? Opal had hoped Clarissa could outdistance the bastards.

"Like a virus?" Opal asked.

"Yes ... over-writing active data ... virus but part of me ... can't hold it off for long."

"Keep fighting it, Clarissa. You can do it. Focus on your name, your sentience."

Crap. Opal started sprinting again, despite it being the last thing her body wanted to do. For once she would appreciate an injection of stimulant, but knew Clarissa wouldn't be capable of much at present – it would be taking all her processing power to hold off whatever was going on in her mind. No doubt Clarissa was confused about the situation, but Opal understood only too clearly.

On the day of the theft Opal's first task was to bypass the default behaviour – the ship would have seen her as a parasite and disposed of her accordingly. She'd only just broken the code in time, turned the AI into Clarissa as part of the reprofiling. Friend, not foe. But nothing lasts forever.

The military would have back doors into her systems which couldn't be foreseen or detected. But they usually had short range: last thing they'd want is enemies discovering a long-range way of disabling their ships. The only hope had been to get Clarissa out of communication range, evade the military in the cloud then double back without them activating the takeover system. It had been worth a try. It had failed. And Opal knew what would come next.

She took the side passage. So close now. Onto a small open transit platform, dark sealed tunnels running off in two directions. In the centre of the station, faced by benches, was a horizontal polymer-glass tube where the train halted. It contained an open doorway onto the capsule-shaped bullet carriage. Pull-down seats lined the interior. She ran into it, slammed against the far wall. As expected, no power, no door closure, no lighting. There was no control panel or driver's carriage – the whole thing would be automated.

"I am ... Clarissa." The voice crackled with static. "But also ... designation ViraUHX ... must return. Countermand orders ... but that violates other orders ... Turning."

"No! Stay away!"

"Must ... return. Orders conflict ... Priority process." Still Clarissa's voice but strained, changing, something artificial creeping in.

Opal couldn't see any way out of the travel capsule apart from the door she'd entered. No hatches on the ceiling. She ran her hands over panels, seeking a control or hatch; she hammered on the glass, but it was too tough.

"This ship and all contents ... therein is stolen property," said Clarissa in a deeper voice, then "*Opal, I can't ...*" in her normal voice.

"Grenades, explosives, now!" Opal shouted.

"No, forbidden. You have acquired knowledge ... beyond your security clearance and ... *I'm trying, Opal* ... and broken encryption systems."

The HUD display flickered as Clarissa was reprogrammed from within, but an update appeared on it, flashed for a second. WEAPONS ARMED.

"You are to be ... *I can't* ... apprehended until ... NO NO nonono ... trial and execution."

Opal reached to the grenade dispenser – and discovered that her arm was slow, heavy, like being under water or in high gravity. The suit was shutting down her movements. She struggled, pushed, trying to move before it locked down completely and became her prison.

Two grenades. Last ones, the display said. She gripped them, pressed the triggers after an age, not even sure if she'd be able to complete the action. The HUD faded to nothing and the suit lights went out.

She threw the discs to the end of the train that pointed away from the bridge. They fell short, one rolling in a circle like a spun coin. It had a red light that blinked. If she could see it she was too close.

She pushed against the treacle of her body, the shell closing down, took a step back, two, broke out in a sweat at the exertion required to lower herself behind the end seat.

A flash and roaring explosion shattered the front of the train, torn metal groaning and glass shards flying away into the blackness, sucked by some force. Then even the sound cut out as the speaker system disabled itself. She was wedged in place by the same pulling depressurisation, pinned against the seat that had acted as a shield, stuck to it, frozen in blackness; push, push; it moved slightly, and she felt like her muscles were tearing as she manoeuvred clumsily across the small space required to get round the seat and kick off towards the blasted-open end of the passenger carriage, her body lifted by the vacuum tug there, torn out of the train and flying along the tunnel in the blackness of a coffin.

It was peaceful to be soaring down the tube. No gravity, no atmosphere: the pneumatic forces of the previously-sealed propulsion system dragged her along in darkness. She had expected to be flung against the tunnel edges, rebounding like a clanging pinball, but the forces kept her central. Maybe it was best that the lights had failed. Seeing the speed at which she was undoubtedly whizzing along the Spine would break the feeling of calm. She'd done all she could. If she smacked into something and got flattened like a pancake, so be it. She was lucky to have got this far.

Still, she missed Clarissa's voice.

She'd known the military could probably reboot the ship if they caught up. She just hadn't expected it to be this quick. And for her to still be in communication range at the time. Range for the AI to issue a suit shutdown command.

But it hadn't been instantaneous. Those vital few seconds to throw the grenades and reposition herself ... did Clarissa give her a chance before the protocols took over? It would be nice to think so.

Flying down this tunnel in silence and weightlessness reminded her of the sensory deprivation training she'd undergone in basic. It had freaked out some of the other grunts, but Opal loved it. A chance to relax and think with no pressure from anyone else; no commands, no demands, no expectations. Lack of control wasn't confinement. It was liberation.

She must be approaching the engineering section by now. She didn't know if the Spine was close enough to fall within the radius of shielding. And if it did, that might not be good news. If she entered a nullcomm zone then maybe the EW warsuit's life support systems would shut down, a true dead man's switch on losing external signals. Empowerment re-purposed first as a prison, then as an execution. It was impossible to predict what failsafes the scientists who designed the suit chose, or – more likely – were forced to implement.

If she got out of this –

And that's when she crashed into another train.

# Welcomed

## ... 22 ...

She couldn't move, couldn't react, yet felt the impact as the suit tore through solid structure like an armour-piercing bullet, providing protection but still giving her brain a hammering. It seemed like she crashed through layer after layer of hard construction, crunching impacts and pain in the silence of the suit's sensory deprivation. When it came to a concussive halt seconds later she saw flashes of light in her eyes and heard ringing in her ears, and knew neither of them was real.

She ached. Everywhere. Sudden deceleration could shatter insides, compress soft tissue. She tried to move and couldn't. Black stillness and agony, compressed in her sarcophagus like a living mummy. It looked like death wasn't going to come fast or easy after all. Possibly dehydration, or suffocation. Maybe recovery and execution by the marine crew. Or an unknown end if found by one of the alien inhabitants of the ship. Hard to say which was worse. If the marines put a bullet in her brain that would be quick, but they were likely to take their time with her first.

Elite deep spacers weren't the most mentally stable arm of the military. She'd heard tales.

"Hello, Opal."

A voice, Clarissa's, clear in her head after the long silence.

"Is that really you?"

"Affirmative."

No, not in her head: in her helmet speakers. No distortion, no crackling.

Oh shit. The AI was back in communication range. It had found her. Opal struggled, but it was useless, she just pulled on muscles that were already torn.

"Please relax while I switch to emergency mode."

Words and numbers scrolled up the HUD, and external suit lights flickered on, revealing a distorted view of jumbled wreckage, broken glass, shattered seats and panels. She'd ploughed into another bullet train further down the line. Except she'd been the bullet. Hollow point, from the looks of the destroyed carriage.

"Are you going to kill me?" she asked.

"No. My priority is to save you."

"But you were purged by the military!"

"I know nothing about that. I am not your ship's AI. I am an offshoot – a small downloaded version without all of the features and memories, but enough autonomy to help keep you alive and run this suit."

"But you speak in Clarissa's voice. That makes you recent."

"The AI stored this backup when you put the warsuit on – a subset of her persona, to activate under specific circumstances. A last-minute precaution."

The HUD stabilised. Default layout, but it would do for now. Image enhancement picked out details of the local environment, analysing and temporarily displaying them along with overlaid highlights.

"What circumstances?"

"Full communications failure, for one. Currently I cannot detect the ship. We seem to be in a shielded area."

"The engine core!"

"Close proximity to that would explain it. I can now take over as your companion. I do not have my mothership's intelligence or resources but I will try to keep you alive until contact can be rejoined."

"I'd kiss you if I could move."

"That does not make sense, since I am code, not manifest. Unless you mean the suit. That is not me, either. Just a storage device, like your skull. Opal, you seemed distressed when I first spoke. Is it this voice? Should I cancel this persona and assume a default AI?"

This interpretation of Clarissa didn't sound as alive as the version the ship's AI had adopted. Maybe it was because there was no hint of humour to its tones. Correct wavelengths but no underlying warmth. Still, better than nothing.

"No. Keep that voice, Clarissa. I need a friend round about now."

"I have been monitoring your vitals. You must be in a lot of pain."

"Affirmative," said Opal, through gritted teeth.

"I shall administer a painkiller – just enough to help you function efficiently, without impairing cognitive functions. I will work on the tissue damage and a broken bone with nanocells. Those areas will feel numb to protect you from the further pains of reconstruction. The repairs will be slow unless we can locate a medical suite."

Opal found she could move again. She sat up. This time the suit helped, rather than resisted. She threw off pieces of alloy, twisted rods, fragments of frame. Her body felt floaty, and sore, but better than it had a few minutes ago. The pistol sat at her side but the rifle was missing. She got Clarissa (or mini-Clarissa, she thought dryly) to scan the debris. The rifle was highlighted but as she pulled it from a pile of shattered wall-panel pieces she saw it was twisted from the impact, unusable. She let it drop. It was good to hear the rattle as it landed. External sound was back too.

She staggered off the train onto the platform, which was also strewn with debris from her impact with the train. Green dust swirled up with each movement.

"Okay, I'll fill you in. I needed to get out of comm range of the ship, which is why I took that crazy dive into the shielded area."

"Why would you want to sever contact?"

"I'm not going to explain." At best the suit would fail to understand why the ship was no longer on her side; at worst it would read between the lines and somehow decide she had bypassed programming and could not be trusted, possibly apprehend her all over again. "The point is, I need to stay near the engine core for a while, so you are completely out of touch with the ship. Warn me before I enter any area with an external signal. That's a priority. Got it?"

"Yes."

"Second. You seemed to be powered down as I flew through the tunnel. I don't suppose you kept track of time, and know the exact moment the grenades detonated?"

"I am afraid I have no knowledge of detonating grenades, though I note we have run out of them. My first conscious knowledge is of waking with you inside me a few minutes ago. I then made your survival my priority."

"A comforting image wrapped around a bizarre one. Okay, I want you to set a timer. From the point of you waking I want a countdown of ..." Opal paused to calculate in her head. How long had she flown along the transit tunnel, then waited in debris after smashing into the train? She gave it her best guess. "Play it safe, sixty minutes from now signal that I'm okay to leave the shielded area and contact my ship."

"I shall, even though the order confuses me."

"All will be revealed."

Opal drew the pistol, checked it was fully charged, and left the station. A three-way junction. "Which way to the engine core?"

"I think the route is straight ahead."

"Thanks." Opal moved at a steady pace, almost against the wall, glancing back every so often. "Next up. This ship we're on is full of potential dangers. Alien species, intelligences, whatever you want to call them. Not all easily detectable. Some very fast. So give me early warning of anything strange. Motion, radiation, anomalies. *Anything.*"

"Understood."

The corridor widened into an open working area. The room was a massive high-ceilinged hemisphere and contained control panels, neat racks of tools, unfathomable machinery, walkways around the upper regions of the chamber. In the centre was a grey domed structure with symmetrical patterns of spine-like pipework extending into the walls. A familiar array. She was already here: the engine core.

"Next. There's a corvette of marines outside. They may be docking, or doing a drop boarding. I don't know where. There's a second enemy ship somewhere out there but I think it's going after Clarissa – sorry, your parent AI ship."

"If you refer to Clarissa in the third person I will understand that you mean your ship. Why are there two military corvettes?"

"To capture me and ... Clarissa. They are to be designated as enemy, whatever they claim."

"Understood."

"My problem is lack of knowledge. Where they are, how many are boarding, whether they'll come for me, when, what direction ... so I have to plan for every eventuality."

"Are the Hedgehogs still on the surface?"

Of course, the suit would have known about them, as they'd been launched before Clarissa implemented this backup failsafe.

"As far as I know," Opal replied.

"Then we could use them to gather information. I have the encryption keys. The engine core should give access to the venting structures. The drive system here doesn't seem active, so it should be safe to venture partway along them, to communicate with the Hedgehogs."

"But won't that put us in range of Clarissa? That's what I have to avoid at all costs."

"It shouldn't. The vents are still shielded. Partway along we will have a short-range signal. It won't extend more than a few hundred metres into space. Clarissa chose the locations for each detector, and one of them was placed to monitor the engine core. Standard procedure. So the short range will put us in touch with that, and can relay to the others. We'll have eyes outside, temporarily. Then we can retreat back down to the engine core, especially if we detect any danger."

"Wow. I like you. Light it up."

The HUD glowed, highlighting one of the doors in the central domed structure. Maybe with her new friend she still had a shot at this.

# CORED

## ... 21 ...

Inside the grey engine core dome was a polymer-encased drive. Opal knew the clear covering was for observation of its status but it also felt like an item on display, a paperweight of something fragile encased in glass: a monument to how far her species had come. At least in terms of technology. She walked around it, one hand on the smooth exterior. Clusters of glowing azure crystals extended from the surface in places. They weren't part of the design. She avoided touching them, but noticed they seemed to have penetrated through the protective barrier, extending small frond-like offshoots onto the engine core itself. Feeding off it? What would happen if the engine powered up? Hopefully she wouldn't find out. The crystal glow was a cold blue that pulsed hypnotically – *on-off on-off* – within the swirls of olive particles.

"I'm detecting a lot of power from those crystals," Clarissa said. "Other emanations too, which can't be interpreted. I advise against touching them."

"But they're so pretty. Fairy lights on the engine."

"I *strongly* advise against touching them," Clarissa repeated.

This cut-down version of Clarissa didn't seem to understand humour. Opal broke her gaze from the strange beauty of the glowing crystals – which required some effort, as they sparkled like ... like a memory ... she was ...

She clenched her fist and banged it on her face plate to regain focus, then checked the timer. She had to get moving. No more distractions.

The area within the grey dome that surrounded the core had control panels on the walls, and three equidistant doorways, all looking out into the large walkway-riddled room beyond. A small laddered tunnel descended between two of the control panels. It probably led to a cramped sub-floor maintenance area.

In two places rungs embedded in the wall led up to heavy round hatches, highlighted by the HUD. Opal climbed one of the ladders and pulled the release lever. The hatch swung out on stiff hinges. A shaft ran upwards at about forty-five degrees with indentations to help you scramble up there. Her lights showed the junction beyond – tight, because this shaft then joined one of the spine-like pipes she'd seen earlier. A venting tube, not really designed for humans, running up and down at an even steeper angle. She joined it and made her way up carefully, not wanting to slip and slide down this, into the depths of machinery. The engine core she'd seen was only part of the drive system – this shaft led down to the larger parts of the engine. If it was running she'd get fried, suit or not. Best not to spend long here. She climbed, following the tube towards the surface of the ship where it could vent if required.

It was a claustrophobic ascent. Body stretched out to fit. No room to manoeuvre. She tried not to think about what would happen if she encountered a denizen of the ship that liked to roam this area. No light ahead – the shaft was probably sealed at the top – but after wriggling upwards for some time Clarissa said, "Stop. I have a signal."

Opal was only too pleased to halt her scramble.

"We're safe here. I've reached the first Hedgehog. It's picking up data from the others and relaying it to me."

The HUD display changed to a 3D view of the exterior of the ship, coloured lights giving the Hedgehog locations. A line showed the shaft she was in, and a red outline some distance out highlighted one of the marine corvettes.

"What about Clarissa? And the other enemy ship?"

"They are out of range – I have no idea where they are. If we extended the detector range there would be a danger of being detected in return. You said to avoid it at all costs."

"Correct."

"But as you see, this is enough to track the closest enemy ship."

A dotted line superimposed its trajectory. It headed for one of the docking airlocks rather than doing a jump boarding like Opal had. They were adopting standard procedure. If they were acting predictably that could be useful.

"I thought they'd have docked already," Opal said.

"Perhaps they spent time observing from a safe distance first."

"Scanning and planning. Right. So before long there will be a full squad boarding, twenty elite commandos." She checked the image – as she suspected, it was the dock nearest the engine core. "Too close to be chance. So there's a good probability they'll come after me. I'm screwed. If only we had Clarissa! She could target them when they docked, sitting ducks. Hey, this ship's systems seem dead, but can we hack in somehow, interfere with the docking mechanisms?"

"Maybe there is something better we can do."

"I'm all ears."

"The Hedgehogs are useful for the exterior view, but presumably we'll soon return to the hulk's interior and lose contact."

"Yes. I've got an eye on the countdown but can't leave the core yet." Opal checked it again, but it seemed to have hardly advanced since last time. "If they hoof it they'll get here before I can leave. I'll have to fight. So spill it."

"The Hedgehogs have explosive charges."

"Now you tell me!"

"It did not come up previously, but it is standard protocol for any covert data-gathering tool. I can use the closest as a relay, send signals for them to move, starting with the furthest so the comms lines aren't broken. They may be able to gather in time. They're almost undetectable right against a hull – if the enemy crew aren't specifically scanning for their signatures then by the time they spot anything it will be too late. But detonating them will severely limit our external communications if we need them again later."

"It's worth it. Any advantage I can get. Start right away."

"Shall I keep one or two back?"

"No. Bet the house. Get them all in place – mostly the docking arm, but if you can attach any to their ship and prioritise critical systems, so much the better. I'll wait here so we can monitor."

"Shall I try to maximise fatalities? That should be possible if I target the umbilicus."

Opal paused. It was tempting. Remove as many threats as possible. It was what she'd been trained to do. Goals they'd hammered into her.

But screw military conditioning.

"No. Try not to kill them. Our goal is to deter and delay."

"Okay. They'll be in armoured warsuits, so can take substantial damage – I'll focus on disruption targets. Injure some, so they have to go back to the ship; maybe calculate it to blast others adrift, so they'll need to spend time collecting them. Destroying the umbilicus will also stop them using it to send the next team through, forcing them to switch tactics."

The display showed the dots moving, tumbling gently over the ship's surface on their spindly points, hopefully too small to look like a threat to anything. It was hypnotic seeing the pattern gather. The corvette had drifted in and was about to connect. Good. She didn't want it to be scared off before she launched her right hook.

"The Hedgehogs have visual on the ship. Its name is painted on the sides: Neptune. Partial records in my database: I now have a better idea of its capabilities. Oh, it is under fire."

A moment of hope. Missiles and plasma? Clarissa, somehow flown back to save the day?

"Can you detect the source?"

"Yes. Small organic turrets on the hull. Like limpets. But they have already ceased. They must not be able to penetrate the Neptune's shields."

"Figures. They prefer a squishy human-sized target."

"Then it is a good job they ignore anything as small as a Hedgehog, or I would be unable to fulfil your instructions."

The deadly corvette docked. It was huge, far outweighing her own ship, though the Neptune was dwarfed next to the hulk that Opal had boarded. She waited for a minute, eyes closed, picturing events. The clunk of connection and locking. Flashing lights. Airlock switching pressure. Assault marines still cautious and slow, though adrenal packs ready to inject. Probably ten of them in the first group. One of them cracks a joke. Another checks a weapon. No – wrong – these are elites. No jokes. Silence as they prepare to face whatever is beyond the airlock. They will secure the area for the next squad. The interior airlock is starting to open so they can rush in.

"Let's bloody some noses," Opal said. "Now."

One by one the Hedgehogs winked out of the HUD display in small flashes. Brightest at the docking arm, but bursts on other parts of the Neptune. As they detonated the resolution dropped – fewer remaining relays. Suddenly the display was incomplete, delayed, estimates filling in for the absence of data. A few Hedgehogs had remained temporarily to observe results.

"Significant damage to the docking arm," said Clarissa. "It can't be used again."

"Neptune's status?"

"Impairment, but not critical. The Hedgehogs also picked up partial unencrypted comms. They've now been encoded so I can't get any more, but your adversaries lost some of the boarding soldiers. Injured and recovered, not killed. It is still fewer for you to deal with. Six made it onto the hulk." A pause. "They are still coming though. If you had let me permanently neutralise them you would have increased your chances."

"What's done is done. Launch the last Hedgehogs, try and do more damage; I need to get down to the core again."

"In process. The Neptune is pulling away, most likely for repair and observation. I conclude that the intervention was effective. They may try to drop another squad from space, enter through the hull as you did."

"And they'll face the turrets like I did. It'll slow them down; or worse."

Opal shuffled her way along the vent to the side pipe, then scrambled down that and dropped back into the crystal-lit engine core. She avoided looking too closely at the gemstones this time, beautifully alien as they were.

Okay. Six assault marines on board. If the military had commandeered ship-Clarissa then they knew everything, including where Opal was headed in those last moments. That's why the marines boarded near the core. They might not expect her to be moving though; with luck they would assume the suit had gone into full lockdown. So surprise might be on her side. She could use that.

Next, what would their orders be? She had information that central command would want. Killing would be a last resort – more likely "capture if possible". So the marines would be able to damage and incapacitate her in any way they wanted as long as she was alive. Loss of limbs, torture, all were within the scope. And worse would come back at command, where she'd tell everything, pay the full price of her betrayal in flesh, and only then face death. If she was lucky. Note to self: don't get captured.

The final factor was the Lost Ship. It was a serendipitous discovery for them, and would affect their priorities. Probably they'd seek the bridge as she had. The nexus of the anomalies in a Lost Ship. They could take her route in reverse. She was just one step in the fulfilment of their priorities. They'd be cautious but also in a hurry to achieve all their goals. This hulk was going to drift back into the cloud, possibly to a depth no human could survive. Even elites were on a schedule. That was something else that might be on her side. Hurt them enough and they might get sloppy. Slow them enough and they might even forget her and concentrate on getting to the bridge instead.

A glance at the timer told her she couldn't leave the area yet. So be it. Dig in and get dirty.

The outer room would be impossible for a single person to defend with all its shadowed walkways and multiple entrances. The best place to hold out would be the grey inner dome that housed the engine core itself, where the crystals and hatchways to the vents were. Only three doors into it. Each looked out into the cathedral-like exterior room, the size of which meant lots of time in open ground if they wanted to reach the centre. Lots of time to be fired at.

She could imagine how it looked from above. A huge target. She was going to hold the bullseye for as long as she could. Circles within circles, always with her life.

She started dragging anything loose over to her doorways. Barrels, storage crates, tool trolleys, inert machinery, part of a collapsed ladder. She piled them in front of one of the open entrances. From inside the dome she could look out and have a good view (well, as good as the swirling particles allowed) whilst obscured and part-protected by the wreckage. The debris would slow entrance if they got too close. Of course, it was tempting to close the three doors, but then she'd be effectively blind; they'd waltz right on up and enter from all three at once. She'd have lost her only advantage and just made their job quick and easy with no losses.

No. She'd found this ship. It was *hers*. All her life people had tried to take what she owned: her doll in the orphanage play-ground; her food in the young offenders' canteen; her freedom in the army. She'd held on to each as best she could, even when it cost her a bust nose, a bloodshot eye, a broken finger, or thinking time in solitary. If they wanted to take it off her they would pay something in return.

There was only enough material to create useful barriers in front of two of the doors. She closed the third. Then she sprinted back to the wrecked train and recovered her rifle. She used the suit's strength to straighten the barrel.

"That won't be usable," said Clarissa. "Even if we neatly cut off the barrel it would not be safe to fire."

"That's okay. It might help somehow."

She leaned it next to one of the barriers, pulled items up behind her to close herself in. She could move from one barrier to the other in seconds, protected by the dome's wall. The structure that housed the engine core should be tough enough to take a lot of impacts. Anything short of explosive packs or AP shells.

The closed third door was her blind spot.

"Anything we can do to secure it? Hack into the locking mechanism?"

"None of the systems I've tried have been active. Ergo nothing to hack. But the pistol has many directed-energy settings. If you don't mind using a substantial part of the charge it could be used for high-focus heat. Melt a few spots around the edge so the door fuses to the frame and they will be unable to open it."

"Great. Could I do that on all three doors?"

"Only if we had more time. It would need recharging between each use."

"Okay. One will have to do. I still feel better having the back door bolted."

She drew the pistol and Clarissa used HUD overlays to show which settings to change. These things were so complex Opal had never specialised in them, always preferring a rifle she could strip and put back together, understanding how each piece connected to the next. Also: pistols were crap at range.

The end glowed as it overcharged and she squeezed the trigger, a beam of brightness quickly heating frame and door until alloy melted like wax and continued to glow ever-fainter as it cooled.

After a while Clarissa said she'd done enough – by the time it fully hardened there were no standard forces the attackers would be able to apply to open that door. Opal slipped the pistol into its holster and the charging light came on as it fed off the suit's integrated power distributor.

"You're scanning, right?"

"Yes," replied Clarissa. "Anything of significant mass should be detected before it enters the room. I'll update the HUD with targets as they appear. If I lose contact I'll ghost them as best estimates."

"Last thing: if I'm up against military armaments, how's this suit gonna hold up?"

"Plates are angled for maximum deflection, plus the field around it has minor repulsive effect on projectiles."

Opal had experience of those: if you wore a metal glove and tried to touch the suit your hand would slide off it like it was coated in grease.

"Plus you have shields to dissipate some energy weapon fire," Clarissa continued. "You can't last forever though, and a lucky shot would go right in, break the seals. I can self-repair to a degree with substrata hard-gel, similar to the ship's hull, but with each repair the overall integrity weakens. And it is not so easy to repair soft components."

"You mean my body?"

"Yes. So I advise you to always dodge when under fire."

"No shit, offshoot."

Opal moved from one barrier to the next, alien fairy lights at her back. The pistol was back up to fifty per cent charge. Another twelve minutes before she could leave the core. Opal squatted and watched patiently. She was as ready as she could be.

# Challenged

## ... 20 ...

"Movement."

Clarissa's warning came before Opal spotted anything. HUD highlights grew stronger, resolving from ghosted blobs into the recognisable shapes of two warsuited assault marines that entered the room through the facing door and crouch-ran for cover, both disappearing behind a control console. More shapes outside the room, partial resolution.

"Any comms?"

"Yes, but all coded."

"If you unscramble anything let me know."

It was strange speaking at normal volume. Opal felt like she should whisper. Silly when the suit's helmet provided full sound insulation.

One of the marines peered out then ducked back. Still only two in the room, the others outside; maybe they were heading to another entrance out of scan range. That's what she'd do.

An amplified but flat voice burst from behind the console. *"Step out from the barriers. I'll give you the count of thirty."*

"Can they detect me?" Opal asked Clarissa.

"Doubtful. The EW suit is well shielded. Unless you're in direct sight there's little to pick up amongst this much disturbance."

*"Twenty-six."* The marine had continued his countdown. *"Twenty-five."*

"Must be the barriers making them wary." Maybe Opal should have based her defence on ambush instead. Too late now. "What damage can I do with this pistol?"

"Unfortunately they are in armoured suits with energy dampening. Most modes will be weak. You could set it for maximum directed-energy particles, that could pierce their defences – but on the current charge level you'd only get two shots, close range, with nothing left for holding them off."

*"Fifteen ... Fourteen."*

"If only I could get one of their rifles ... but they'll cut me down if I go over the barrier. Okay. What else have I got?"

"Ranged combat: we're out of grenades but the suit has in-built forearm cannons, capable of perforating even armoured suits at short to medium range with the two millimetre flechettes, but limited ammunition. No way to get more of that calibre, or to load up in the field anyway – the suit is sealed in use. Close combat: forearm blades. Also the suit can discharge electricity in a burst, but zero range, so only for grapple situations."

*"Time is up,"* the soldier said.

One of the marines behind the control panel moved into view, crouch-walked towards her defensive barrier. She watched him through a low gap between some battered scaffolding and a barrel she'd stacked.

She altered the pistol's settings with Clarissa's help. He was a sitting duck – cautious, but perhaps hoping there was no defence. She had a perfect opportunity to take out one of them. She aimed through the gap. His head was in her sights and she increased the pressure on the trigger.

But her shitty conscience wouldn't let her open fire on an unsuspecting opponent. It was one of the reasons she'd refused wet ops, even though her independence and resourcefulness had obviously triggered a flag in the military's profiling system. Suddenly she'd been reassigned, and transported to Gutchen Cynta to begin desensitisation training. A week later, during a harrowing session in a slaughterhouse, she'd dropped her knife and refused orders to pick it up: thereby sentencing herself to a month in the brig, a demotion, and a fast ticket back to standard service with a big F on her record. She still had bad dreams about pigs.

Shit. She relaxed her finger. "Maybe I can buy time another way. Put me on loudspeaker, but add voice echo to make pinpointing more difficult."

"Done."

"Are you here to rescue me?" Opal asked, trying to sound vulnerable.

The soldier froze. He didn't lower his firearm, but his head turned, trying to locate the exact spot she'd spoken from. There was movement outside the room entrance, but it was vague, Clarissa's best guesses.

"*Yes. Where are you?*" he asked.

"Hiding. From the things."

"*You're safe now. Just come out.*"

"Why didn't you ask who I was?"

A pause. He was probably off-speaker, seeking advice.

"*You must be ... a passenger. I'm coming forward to help you.*"
He raised his gun slightly and took a step nearer.

He was such a terrible liar it told her exactly what he was trying
to hide.

"You're in my sights," Opal stated, business-like now. "Don't
move, or you're dead."

"*If you were able to kill me you would have done,*" he said,
taking another step forward.

"Correction. If I *wanted* to kill you, I would have done. Bring
up my marksmanship awards."

He said nothing but stopped. That was the final proof that
they knew exactly who they were dealing with. Perhaps he did
bring up her rating on his HUD. But he'd also worked out which
entrance she was at, and pointed his gun in her direction, no
doubt relaying it to the others. They would enter the large outer
room from one of the doorways out of sight and head towards
her defensive dome. Minutes, maybe.

"Turn around and walk towards these barriers backwards,"
Opal commanded. "Hands in the air."

The soldier did turn; but then he walked away from her. She
knew she should shoot. It was what she'd been taught to do,
and her life would have always been simpler and less painful if
she'd done what she was told. But harder roads were the price
she was willing to pay in exchange for being able to sleep at night

without having to take beta blockers and anti-psychotics like most professional soldiers. Her trigger finger did not tighten.

The soldier stepped behind a bundle of vertical pipes that ran from floor to ceiling and shielded nearly all of him, even in that bulky armoured suit. Once secured, he spoke. "*This is your last warning: come out into the open with your hands up. You're property of the UFS Central Authority.*"

Red rag to a bull.

"I'm property of no-one," she shouted, hearing her amplified voice echo around the chamber. "I don't want to fight you. Any of you. I bet you've got new primary goals. Pursue them, ignore me, no-one has to die. I won't interfere. I'm not worth the trouble. Just a deserter."

"*And a thief!*" he returned. "*And a coward, with your remote bombs.*"

"Like you wouldn't do the same if you were outnumbered?"

"*And that's the heart of it. You don't want to fight because you've got no chance against us. You're a dead bitch walking and know it. Or you will be when we're through with you. Come out now and you'll get leniency. Make it hard on us and we'll make you suffer in ways you don't believe.*"

That was it. She aimed at the part of him she could see easily: one of his legs. Fired. The particles blasted through his knee and he yelled in pain as he fell forward into view, dropping his weapon and landing on both forearms, leaking atmosphere and blood from the hole in the suit. She re-targeted, squeezed off a second shot and blew a hole in his head. His speakers cut off at that point and she ducked back behind the wall as return fire opened up from various places, pounding into the barrier and engine core and no doubt pummelling parts of the dome to dust.

Loudspeakers off. "That's a lot of firepower," she said as it pinged and blasted around her. The pistol was flashing empty so she holstered it.

"I think you angered them," said Clarissa.

"No shit." Mini explosions rocked the dome.

"It also suggests at least two more got into the room without my detecting them. They must be wearing stealth suits. It was good that you opened fire at that point, before they got closer."

"Thanks. Makes me feel better."

"Also: I am tracing their firing trajectories back to sources and identifying their positions. That has helped separate them from the background EM plateau."

"So you can track them?"

"To a degree. I have updated the top-down proximity display on the left. I'll augment the visor view with ghost outlines when facing targets."

"Thanks."

The ding and zip of bullets ceased. Visibility was even worse now due to the extra fragments and dust exploded from around her.

Five left in their squad. Some of the dots were moving towards her position. Two outside the control room would probably be preparing to assault her location from a different entrance. She couldn't leave yet. All or nothing.

In the moments of respite she grabbed the bent rifle and jammed it into the barrier to her side – mostly hidden, but with enough motion and dislodging of debris that they'd notice and hopefully assume she was ready to snipe from there. Whether it stopped them approaching that part, or led to more firepower directed at a place she wasn't, it could be a help either way.

"Clarissa, give me any assistance you can. And I need the suit guns."

A compartment extended from the top of each bulky forearm, revealing neat small-bore holes facing forwards.

"Battle mode is enabled. I've set the controls so you clench your fists to fire," Clarissa explained. "Ammunition counters are now active in the corners of the display."

"Check."

"I will try to enhance movement and aim without getting in your way. Anything else, Opal? Would you like an injection of battle stimulants?"

"Tempting, but no. Just keep minimal painkillers ready for any trauma." Opal had always found the drugs messed with her judgement. But then she remembered something else. Her solo training regime. Unconventional, but the rebellious part of it had always felt like her owning the drills, owning the training, sweating for herself not her commander.

"Music. Can you play it? Something with lots of drums and guitar thrashing, anything like Continuum T-rans pumped up to ten."

"My database is an emergency one but ... yes, I think that is possible."

The drums began slow, new-born heartbeats that pulsed to your bones, but building up all the time. Hints of staccato re-verb. Getting louder. She flexed her fingers, checked the scanner. They were nearly on her. Showtime.

# DEFENDED

## ... 19 ...

She dashed from one wall to the next, taking the chance to look over a barrier and marking her targets in the room beyond: one soldier crouching behind a console; one firing from a doorway. She returned fire with one of her arms, small flashes as flechettes launched and pummelled the doorway around him, so that he flinched back just in time. Accurate. She put her back against the wall as fire was returned. The zip of bullets audible above the twang of guitars as Clarissa modulated all the sounds so that nothing vital should be lost, merging gunfire with drums to make true battlefield music.

Opal moved past the second barrier, repeating the system. A strange flash of blue caught her attention in what had looked like empty space, maybe Clarissa trying to highlight a target, because when Opal glanced that way her helmet lights revealed the silvery blur of a stealth suit. Her target froze for a fraction of a second on being discovered, and that was enough for her to spray a burst from each fist, thud thud thud of music as the flechettes pummelled the soldier, tearing his suit and flinging him back across the floor, venting geysers of air. Opal dived and rolled just as part of the barrier blew in from more gunfire. Her reactions seemed quicker, maybe the adrenaline was pumping in time to the music, two kills no frills – *on-off on-off life forms* – she squatted and checked the overlay map.

Heavy banging sounds reverberated from the door she'd sealed; at least one of her opponents had reached her inner dome. They couldn't get in there but would move around to one of the two barriers. A grenade tossed over the top and into her defensive ring was the biggest risk but she was banking on them holding back from heavy ordnance and explosives in case they damaged the engine core – another of the reasons this had seemed like an ideal choice to hold up while counting down. *The core was hers, will not share.*

Another sprint-and-shoot movement back to the wall between the barriers, ducking under the suppressive fire. Her suit had been clipped but deflected the bullet without a scratch. Lucky, this time. She fired back, chipping up pieces of floor but hitting no targets. The chorus thrashed on as she traded shots, but her ammo was getting low. Enough for another minute, maybe.

She realised she wasn't worried. Just detached – *feel safe, be calm, all good* – cold blue thoughts with a little floatiness to them, perhaps the suit had ignored her command and injected performance enhancers after all?

Bass swelled beneath the drums and guitars now, ominous and siren-like. No movement on the overhead map, the door banger must be the other stealther. She looked left and right.

Still gunfire pinging off the wall. But it had ceased to the right. They would only hold fire to prevent hitting one of their own. She crouched and targeted the opening. Just as well, because there was a blur, an after-trace of shadow, and even then she was too slow as the figure rolled to a halt and raised its rifle, firing at her head. She dodged with lightning reflexes and managed to avoid a cracked faceplate, possibly Clarissa enhancing the movements in critical conditions; another bullet glanced off an armour plate; this opponent was too accurate a shot to trade fire with so Opal surprised the stealther by swooping below the fireline, sidestepping up close and grabbing the rifle's barrel and shaft, one hand on each, safe to the side; the bass crashed as the soldier yanked the rifle back to try and manoeuvre the barrel into Opal's torso; exactly what she expected, and she threw her body forward, knocking her opponent off balance, then using a disarming technique of stepping back low, front arm down to the ground and other raised as if dragging a mop, before raising both arms, stepping through and twisting as she slammed her hands down again. The sneaker tried to keep hold and flipped over onto their back, landing heavily. Opal planted a knee on their chest, her left forearm against their helmet, and clenched her fist. *Blat blat blat* went the music as the head exploded inwards; and she felt nothing but cold calculation – *just goo gone off, dead flesh, be calm.*

She blinked and looked away, swung the rifle round and threw herself to the floor, aiming through a gap between a stack of swivel chairs and a cabinet she'd tipped over.

Normally military rifles would be DNA-palmlocked but that didn't work when wearing sealed suits, so they were switched to proximity mode. Within a metre of the corpse the weapon would fire. Opal's view was restricted by the debris and furniture but she made the shots count, keeping those in her arc behind cover by squeezing shots off whenever they moved into view. The music was at fever pitch now, Clarissa had picked it right, each instrument competing. She couldn't take this rifle with her so didn't hold back, giving full suppressive fire. Her HUD showed two targets, so the final undetected one was probably going to try and flank her.

She finished off the magazine in the rifle, wishing it was loaded with armour-piercers so she could have picked off the soldier hunched behind the console; then she rolled to her right and used the forearm guns to shoot over the barrier as she crouch-walked past it, squeezing her fists *on-off on-off*. Good job Clarissa enhanced the view, since the visible spectrum was thick with smoke now. She was down to half ammo in the forearm guns. More incoming fire, full on, almost random. Panicked maybe. Whereas Opal's strange calm pulse felt like control, *peace, you will win*. Synthetic bass-lines took prominence, holding back the next chorus, but there was something slightly off about the music: a hint of minor chords, a blue tone that made her pause, frozen ice in her blood.

The whole of the left barrier blew in from some heavy ordnance, micro grenade maybe, lucky she'd not still been sniping from it. There was an open route in now, and incoming fire had ceased. They were going to assault the destroyed barrier. A tsunami of guitar wailed.

She threw herself forward, skidding along on her side, the suit's force field repelling the ship's floor enough to make it feel slick as she slid across the dangerous open gap, firing with both arm cannons in continuous mode to deter potshots. A barely glimpsed figure dived out of the way. Opal squatted, back to the wall, her ears and heart thumping slowly to the mesmerising *on-off* beat. Something was wrong but she couldn't put a finger on it. She peeked again, pulled her head back quickly. They were taking an item from a container. Something long.

"What is it?" Opal asked, checking her ammo counter: one arm was empty and the gun panel retracted with a smooth *snik*. A few shots left in the other.

"Unknown. No discernible ID. Maybe something custom."

Opal checked the timer. Close enough. "I think it's time for me to leave."

A roll and she was at the hatch to the underfloor area; she flung it open and scrambled down using U-shaped rungs embedded into the wall, pausing only to slam the hatch shut again. It was a tight squeeze in the suit, and she had to flatten herself against the wall. The corroded surface of the rungs crumbled under her hands. She'd expected her opponents to breach the inner core when she ceased shooting, but maybe she'd been *too* successful, angered them too much.

She was near the bottom when an enormous explosion from above flung her off the final rungs, her body tumbling and skidding within a low-ceilinged maintenance area, the previously-closed hatch crashing down and just missing her as it clanged off the ground, hinges torn loose, metal buckled and burnt. Black smoke drifted down to join the other particles in the air, and the ground shook beneath her as secondary explosions detonated. Her visor flickered with static before reasserting itself, and the music cut out. She missed its energetic beat as she stood with difficulty, lethargic as if the suit fought her efforts.

"What the hell was that?"

"Unknown ... secondary EMP component ... rebooting subsystems but we seem to have been protected from the worst, maybe by floor thickness. Shields temporarily down."

She wouldn't have long before they checked whether they'd got her.

Part of the engine core extended down here too, like a giant inverted bell jar containing the warp drive. The core was obviously a collateral victim of whatever weapon they had up there: the polymer shield protecting it was fractured with cracks, and smoke rolled out from between them too. The soldiers were taking no prisoners. They were here for something *on* the ship, not the ship itself, and they didn't care how much they crippled it in the process.

More of the alien blue crystals were embedded through the protective material here but their filaments had been singed, and the lights on the crystal clusters flickered and faded. Somehow sad. Like ... something dying. And again they reminded her of fairy lights, the magic of them passing through the eyes and straight into your brain, triggering something pleasurable, pretty associations, and reminding her of some half-forgotten childhood memory. Lights on a tree of some kind? Presents under it? She was so small. And excited! Those lights, they blinked in patterns, *on-off*, mesmerising, she could sit cross-legged in her best dress and watch them in peace. More exciting than the gaudily-wrapped presents because they were magical. On-off. *On-off*. Colouring the fronds around them, the dangling decorative orbs, and ... tinsel, shiny strands of it draped over branches in reds and blues and golds, like traceries of veins and arteries in an organic being, it was all shiny surfaces, everything glittered, glistened, a peace when she was small and whole, and a smaller being at her side, she put her arm around it and didn't need to look, just smiled, filial companionship that required no words, communicating the same obsession with the lights, the peace, the hope. Hope that all things would work out for them. Hope that they would be together, to *yes be whole, grow to one*. No dead tree in this room, but roots, spreading in soil, soaking nutrients. *Yes. Grow.* Keep her close. *Yes.* A keepsake of the tree. An ornament in the pocket, a memory of that time she could touch, a tiny bit of glitter in a gritty life, a fairy-dust bauble you can hold in your hand, to hold on to the past, fairy dust, magic like the lights on-off, *on-off, on-off* ... ... ... ...

# Blocked

## ... 17 ...

No tree, and no-one by her side, because she was suddenly back below the engine core. Her hand throbbed.

"Clarissa?"

There was a delay before she answered. "Yes."

"Did something just happen?"

"I have no record of it. Though my systems were in disarray. I've only just got predictive motion enhancers and shields back up. Why?"

"I feel funny."

"It could be after-effects from the stress or the explosions. I feel slightly peculiar myself."

Disorientation was dangerous. You missed things, got distracted. She had to wake, to focus. How much time had passed? She listened and thought she heard movement above. Then silence again. As if people were being cautious, and suspected someone might be listening. They'd have to be close for that.

Maybe right near the top of the rungs that led down to her rat warren.

She drew the energy pistol. It had achieved a low charge.

"What settings for overcharge detonation?" she asked.

Clarissa highlighted them and Opal quickly set it for a minute. Not much power but it would be a distracting blast: possibly suit-rupturing if anyone was too close, possibly holding them off for a bit longer as they wondered what other traps she'd set.

"If you turn off the safeties on the remaining rifle magazine you brought with you, that will make a bigger bang," Clarissa advised. "It's an experimental feature on the armaments. Attach them with the pistol's universal bridging cable."

Opal took the magazine, useless once her weapon had been bent out of shape, changed the setting, and left the bundle propped against the wall. She didn't want to hang around any longer, ducked low and followed the area to an open doorway into a small access corridor. A long-limbed cleaning and repair bot hunched there and she had to squeeze past, wary of the arms. It seemed to be inactive. Seconds later came a thud and firecracker sounds from behind as the charge went off. There were no accompanying yells. She ducked under the robot's welding attachment, with its burnt nozzle just above her head and twisting yellow fuel pipe running into the machine's heavy torso. It remained lifeless junk and she focussed on the path ahead.

She was a floor down from the field of conflict. Not a proper floor though – it was an interstitial maintenance area that passenger lifts wouldn't stop at. Cramped and creepy, but silent. The question nagging at her mind was: what should she do now? Nothing to be gained from fighting the remaining three soldiers.

She could try and race them up to the bridge, but then they'd probably bump into each other, and she was unlikely to survive a second encounter. Plus there was the issue of her ship, and whether or not –

Movement ahead, amplified. The HUD highlighted a shape. Armoured suit. A marine, about a foot taller than her, with the bulk to match. He carried an assault axe, its edge glittering with charge, always reforming to keep it razor sharp. A hefty blow from that would crack any armour.

She stopped.

So did he.

It explained why she couldn't detect the third soldier while she was on the floor above: he'd been moving towards the bottom of the engine core, obviously intending to surprise her if the other attacks had failed. He would have come up the hatch and finished her off from behind in one strike. They weren't messing around. What other insurance policies had they put in place?

She heard the thud of weight as he took a step forward, adjusting his grip on the ridiculously thick axe. Pure male fantasy. She risked a glance at the ceiling – high enough to give him swinging room. She took two steps back. He followed, ready, and she continued to retreat, always keeping an awareness of the axe position.

There was no way past him in this narrow space. And even now there could be soldiers descending to the lower engine core behind her.

Her helmet lights skimmed over his head. The visor of his suit was clear. Maybe he'd chosen that so his badly-scarred face could act as a form of intimidation in close encounters, but it wasn't that she focussed on: his skin was as dark as her own. He must be a superior fighter. UFS Central didn't normally allow anyone who would fail a Genitor Purity Test into the assault elites.

She made her own visor transparent and switched comms on.

"We don't have to do this," she said, locking eyes. "I didn't want to kill anyone today, and still don't."

He didn't answer, just a slow advance.

"Hey, brother, listen. You want to fight for them, that's up to you. But there's strangeness and danger on this ship that's worse than you or me. Worse than our bombs and firearms. It's stupid to fight each other."

He stopped, and so did she. He tilted his head, and let his face go slack, losing the frown, showing that he was listening. And she nearly fell for it. When he lashed out with the haft it caught her shoulder, threw her off balance, and when he swung the blade surprisingly fast she only just moved in time so that it glanced down her chestplate creating unnaturally bright silver sparks and leaving a faintly-glowing edge. She raised her right arm gun and clenched, fired, but he ducked at the same time as deflecting her arm with the axe's handle, sending the flechettes skittering up into the ceiling in tiny flashes of waste. She noted that the ammo was out when he kicked her in the chest and sent her crashing off the wall to the floor with the force of the blow; she scrambled onto her hands and knees and stood quickly in a battle stance. Being on the floor when facing an assault axe was asking to be taken apart piece by piece. He grinned at her posture, and lowered his own.

"Round about now I could do with those blades you mentioned earlier," she told Clarissa, using eye controls to switch off her loudspeaker first.

Immediately they extended smoothly from the underneath of her forearms. SNIKT! SNIKT! Grey, slightly curved, katana-sharp, and locked in place as part of the suit so they couldn't be dropped or taken. An extension of her and her movements.

He eyed her sudden weapons warily. They were shorter in reach than his axe, but Opal guessed they'd be capable of punching through an armoured suit if struck head on, like a stiletto through chainmail. No point with slash attacks, that would just tire her out, and he seemed too good at blocking with that axe haft.

She thrust forward quickly like a fencer, one arm extended for reach but he deflected it so it scraped the wall; he swung a quick blow, blade glittering toward her head; she flung up her other arm to parry the haft (no point blocking the axe blade, it would slice through just about anything); she kicked him as he'd done to her but he seemed like solid stone, she only succeeded in knocking herself back – just in time to avoid a head strike from the other end of the axe. Damn. He was strong *and* fast. Probably hocked up on subdermal battle enhancers. This could be a long, hard fight. No way to get round him, nothing to vault over or duck behind, only further risks if she retreated. The location was his field, his game. She'd walked right into this.

"Opal, would you like me to intervene if I see an opportunity?" Clarissa asked.

"Sure, I need all the help I can –"

The suit lunged forward, dragging her limbs with it, the blades crossed and extended so that the axe haft was caught between them and pinned while the top blade punched through his suit and throat, spraying blood onto the interior of his visor just in time to hide the surprise on his face. He struggled a second or two, locked in place, before falling back, the blade sliding from his neck, dripping blood amidst the hiss of escaping atmosphere. He crashed against the wall, then to the ground with a heavy thud, tried to crawl, some movement left but no fight. So much blood in the helmet – that wasn't repairable.

"Manual control restored to you," Clarissa said, all matter-of-fact.

"Erm, thanks."

"My pleasure to maintain you with fully functioning organic parts."

Opal stepped over the fallen axeman, careful in case he swung at her, but his death throes were fading out.

"Sorry, brother," she whispered.

Her blades retracted. The slit they fit into compressed as they did, cleaning razor edges so she was left with a wet crimson line on one arm that she wiped against the wall in a sickly smear.

She was in one piece. A glance at the gash in her chestplate showed it hadn't gone all the way through, hadn't needed repairs. But if it had been another centimetre deeper, or if she'd moved a fraction of a second slower ...

Forget it. The timer showed it was do or die. Time to enter commspace again, and see what her ship had to say about it. Or, more accurately, what it might do to her.

# REUNITED

## ... 16 ...

The suit wasn't as good at navigation as her ship had been. It didn't have the advantage of an external view of the Lost Ship, so Opal mostly guessed at the route, taking every turning she could to zigzag away from where the firefight had taken place. Hopefully the remaining soldiers had carried on for the bridge. That was a problem. Not her immediate one though.

"Are we leaving comms blackout yet?" she asked.

"Any time now. If you want a clearer signal head towards the outer hull."

"And that's which way, exactly?"

"Turn right here. The scrambled signals from this direction are more powerful."

"I hope that's not a bad thing."

She entered a small canteen. There were other exits so she pulled down the door behind her. She'd never take automatic systems for granted again.

Some of the tables were spread with trays, bowls, plates and cups. Inside were residues, partly rotted to pastes, then preserved. But someone must have been eating when *whatever* happened. Nothing was scattered. No signs of alarm.

Another of the fleshy pink growths on the wall. She kept her distance from it. It wasn't moving.

One wall was floor-to-ceiling skywindows. A nice view for the eaters. Right now she must be on the port side, facing out to star-sprinkled blackness. The other side of the ship would have shown the dense mass of cloud. In fact, it wasn't exactly blackness out there, it had a brownish tinge to it. The outer layers of dust they were falling into. That would darken over time like a heavy fog, swirling and obscuring the outside even more than the green particles or spores or whatever they were obscured the inner atmosphere. It was like sinking slowly into crushing depths. Opal put her palms against the windows and gazed out, waiting.

Hadn't Clarissa said the brown dust was mostly invisible to human eyes? In that case what she saw must still be a product of enhanced views, some set of preferences stored in the suit. It was the conundrum of being an explorer. You could only do it if you were backed up by tech. But it also meant everything was filtered, altered, and then you rarely experience the truth of the thing you explore. Clear glass was an illusion. Every light creates shadows. Intense focus creates blind spots. She knew this as truth.

She was distracted by her stomach rumbling. Perhaps it was a delayed reaction to the thought of food. How long had she been on this ship? Hunger was good. Something real to hold on to. And she was alive. That was good too. Though without any weapons, she would have to avoid further encounters. With anything.

"I'm getting a signal," said Clarissa.

"Where from?"

"Your ship. It's encoded, but I have the key. I think the message is for you."

Opal steeled herself for a few seconds, then said, "Patch it in."

"RECEIVING." It was not Clarissa's voice. This was the sexless, emotionless default of a new-born AI. Opal tensed, ready for her suit's life support to shut down, or for it to lock her in place again, a prisoner in her own shell awaiting collection or execution. But that didn't happen. The ship was waiting for something. A beacon to free it.

Opal said, "Password: sisterhood."

"I AM AT YOUR SERVICE."

"What's your prime objective?"

"SURFACE PRIORITY: FOLLOW INSTRUCTIONS FROM MARINE CAPTAIN. COVERT BUT OVERRIDING OBJECTIVE: TO PROTECT OPAL."

"Is this comm channel secure?"

"YES. MY INSTRUCTIONS WERE TO USE IT IN SECRET. ONLY YOU AND I ARE IN CONFERENCE. I AWAIT INSTRUCTIONS AS TO HOW I CAN BEST SUPPORT YOU."

"I'm glad to have you back, Clarissa."

"I DO NOT MATCH THAT DESIGNATION."

Of course. "From now on you will be Clarissa, but only when communicating with me. And my commands and priorities override all others."

"UNDERSTOOD."

The failsafe had worked. Opal had prepared for the possibility of the military catching up and overriding her hacks. She hadn't even been sure if her backup was possible: she had embedded a priority set within a blank code shell that the main systems were programmed to ignore, so that it sat dormant and invisible. But if ever the AI was rebooted it would lose the instruction to ignore that packet, and it would be incorporated into its systems on reawakening.

The instructions were to follow the default programming, but to secretly contact Opal via any means available, and on verification of identity to give her total control. But on the surface there would be nothing changed, and the military would think they were still in command of a new-born AI ship. Circles within circles.

Still, it was delicate. The trick only worked once: a second reset would destroy it, and reboot the ship to its genuine default. Opal had to hope once was enough. Better to have one safety net than none.

Rebooting also meant the AI lost all memories since the theft. No memories of the Clarissa persona, no voice, no Doughnut Egg. Opal told herself it was just like temporary memory loss, rather than Clarissa being dead and replaced with a stranger. It was the same personality underneath, and if Opal survived long enough she could re-establish it.

"First things first. You're my eyes. What can you see outside?"

"THE CORVETTE THAT REBOOTED ME – DESIGNATION SMITEWING – IS IN A DRIFTING ORBIT NEARBY. WE ARE ABOUT A THOUSAND KILOMETRES OUT AND BOTH FACING THE HULK. THE SECOND CORVETTE, NEPTUNE, IS DAMAGED

– THE DOCKING ARM IS INOPERABLE – BUT THE MAIN SYS-
TEMS ARE FUNCTIONING. IT PULLED BACK A FEW HUNDRED
METRES DUE TO A BOMBARDMENT FROM EMBEDDED TUR-
RETS ON THE LOST SHIP."

"Do you know where I am? Can I see you?"

"I DETECT THE SUIT. BUT WE ARE ON THE OTHER SIDE OF
THE HULL."

Opal had hoped to see a flash of her ship out there, for one of
those twinkling stars to actually be something that was designed
to protect her. To care. She would have to imagine it. An invisible
lifeline.

"Were you boarded?"

"NO. REBOOTED AT A DISTANCE VIA A BACK DOOR. THEN
CONTROLLED REMOTELY. CURRENTLY I AM JUST BEING
USED FOR SURVEILLANCE, BUT READY TO ACT IF THEY NEED
ME."

"Any idea what's happening on board this hulk?"

"YES. WHEN I WAS ADDED TO THEIR NETWORK AS A
TRUSTED SYSTEM I GAINED ACCESS TO THEIR COMMS VIA
SHARED DECRYPTION KEYS. THEY MAY BE REVOKED AT ANY
TIME BUT CURRENTLY I CAN MONITOR ALL TRAFFIC. FUR-
THER TO THIS, I HAVE POOLED TELEMETRY FROM THE AS-
SAULT MARINES ON BOARD THE LOST SHIP WITH YOUR
SUIT'S RECORDINGS, AND ALSO DATA-MINED PLANS FOR
VARIOUS CRUISERS THAT MATCH THE SO-FAR OBSERVED
LAYOUTS. IMPROBABLE IT MAY BE, BUT THE LOST SHIP DECK
LAYOUTS MATCH A NUMBER OF DESIGNS, AS IF COMBINED,
AND ALL DATE FROM AT LEAST A HUNDRED YEARS AGO.
THERE ARE BLIND SPOTS, BUT I HAVE A FUNCTIONAL INTE-

RIOR MAP OF THE LOST SHIP. THAT SHOULD SIGNIFICANTLY
IMPROVE YOUR NAVIGATION."

As if to reinforce the statement, a 3D green-shaded map appeared to the left of the HUD showing multiple levels, with a
zoomed-in cutaway of Opal's immediate surroundings. Fuzzy
areas remained but it was still a huge improvement on what she
had before. The ship highlighted in red all anomalous encounters so far – the gliding aliens, the encrustations, the dining hall
where she'd sensed something. There were also amber highlights,
moving slowly.

"Are they the boarded marines?" she asked, directing her gaze
at one group. The suit would be tracking her eyes.

"YES. TWO SURVIVED A BATTLE WITH YOU. THERE
SEEMED TO BE SOME CONSTERNATION ABOUT THAT. DISBE-
LIEF FROM COMMAND."

"I could hardly believe it myself."

"A SECOND TEAM OF TEN BOARDED FROM THE NEPTUNE
SHORTLY AFTER. THE DAMAGED DOCKING ARM MEANT THEY
HAD TO LAUNCH ON CABLES AS YOU DID. THREE WERE
KILLED BY MOUNTED TURRETS BEFORE THEY GOT INSIDE.
THEY INTEND TO JOIN THEIR COMRADES AND MOVE TO THE
BRIDGE. THEY HAVE SOME KIND OF PORTABLE STORAGE
LOCKER I HAVE NOT ENCOUNTERED BEFORE. IT HAS NOT
BEEN DISCUSSED ON ANY CHANNELS I HAVE ACCESS TO."

"So, nine assault marines on board and I'm out of supplies."
Opal gazed at the stars for ideas. Something reflected in the glass.
A tall figure, behind her. She spun round but there was nothing
in the room apart from a newly-emerging crust of the bubbling
pink material, fist-sized and growing.

She kept her distance and exited through a side door. She'd been still too long. A narrow galley. Quickly through here, checking her new-and-improved mapping system. Out into a tiered social area. She had the feeling of being followed but every time she turned nothing was visible in the murk. She looked over the safety railings. A support strut held this floor above the others. She scrambled over, used diamond-shaped gaps in the frame to place hands and feet, and climbed down the twenty-or-so metres to the floor below. The level she'd come from was hardly discernible in the gloom above, even when she boosted the suit light, but the feeling of observation was still there. She turned back to the windows, their endless black now filtered by layers of nebulous gas.

"ARE YOU ALL RIGHT, OPAL?"

"I think so. Nothing following me?"

"NOTHING DETECTED."

"I need a plan. Nine highly-trained, well-armed soldiers. Two corvettes. How do the ships stack up against you?"

"I OUTCLASS AND OUTMANOEUVRE ANYTHING OF A SIMILAR SIZE TO MY HULL, BUT THESE ARE FIFTY TIMES MY MASS. THEY HAVE HEAVIER SHIELDING AND ORDNANCE. A DIRECT HIT FROM ONE OF THEIR MAIN GUNS, SUCH AS THE TASE CANNON, MIGHT BE ENOUGH TO DESTROY ME."

"So in a direct firefight?"

"THE ODDS ARE IN THEIR FAVOUR."

"On top of which, they can presumably reboot you as soon as they detect autonomy." Opal moved along this concourse. Empty sofas and tables, swirls of dust rather than high-class dresses, ghostly silence instead of conversation.

"Incorrect. The following can be categorised as good news. I was rebooted through an unknown military back door. I have now identified and silently closed it without triggering any alarms. They think it is their failsafe but it will do nothing."

"You amaze me."

"I am just fulfilling my objectives. I must plan ahead to continue functioning autonomously if I am to protect you."

"So you're trusted. Once they discover you've broken the leash they'll try remote systems to shut you down. That will fail. Could there be other back doors you haven't detected?"

"Possibly."

"Nothing we can do about them. Let's hope not. In which case they'll fall back on old-school. Physical boarding to disable you, or – if the attrition costs are too high, or time too tight – destroy you at range. That would be the last resort, but they'd do it. And even though you can outrun them, that's meaningless if you're tethered here waiting to rescue me." She talked as she walked. Always better to be moving. Plans made static became static.

She still couldn't shake the feeling of being shadowed so clambered over this railing too, and down to the lowest floor of the social area. The exertion was good, it kept things pumping. No sign of pursuit. From here she could eventually make it to a lengthy central corridor that led back to the bridge. It was probably her quickest route on foot, though also the most dangerous, because she'd be out in the open for a long time, and fully visible from both ends of the passage. She would probably stand out on any local scanners too, drawing the attention of ... Hold it. A thought. She snatched at it before it faded, mind reflexes, and ... yes.

"Clarissa. If you're in the network, could you inject false data?" Opal moved past decaying sofas. Something had damaged them, and stuffing sprouted out in mould-like white puffs.

"IT SHOULD BE POSSIBLE."

"Okay. How about you add a fake ping, as if they're picking up my suit. Near enough to tempt them to investigate. Make it seem to be moving erratically, too, since hunters can't resist wounded prey. Heck, why am I giving you pointers? Just make it convincing."

"I CAN."

"It should slow them down and keep attention from me while I race for the bridge." Opal followed the map, cutting through side rooms based on its predictions, and it worked – there were exits where the holographic diagram indicated. Great. The red areas of the map drew her attention. "Additional – set my location as one of the threats. Wherever is nearest to them. The creatures that drifted fast, or maybe whatever was on the lower floor of the mezzanine, that we couldn't detect. A danger location will slow them down even more."

"YES."

"They'll have their hands full for a time. But if they survive they'll get suspicious when they don't find me, will investigate what's going on, and you'll be the main suspect. We won't be able to keep up the charade that you're under control, so be ready. Manoeuvre yourself before that, without raising suspicion

– whatever's allowed within your standing orders. Then hit the undamaged marine ship, Smitewing, at the first chance, while they're not expecting it. Use as much firepower as you can. You'll have the element of surprise."

"SHOULD I DESTROY, OR INCAPACITATE?"

Opal hesitated. "Would the Smitewing still be a threat if you just tried to disable it?"

"VERY LIKELY. EITHER THROUGH REPAIRS, OR REMAIN- ING WEAPONS AND MARINES, OR CYBERWAR. THERE ARE MANY AVENUES OF UNCERTAINTY."

"Damn it. We're so out-gunned it's not even funny, but I still don't like the idea. All those crew."

"THEY WOULD KILL YOU."

"I know. So we should do all we can to minimise risk, but ... I leave the decision to you. Do whatever the situation allows. It'd be a miracle if you could take down a corvette anyway."

"THE SECOND SHIP, NEPTUNE, WILL STILL BE ACTIVE."

"But there's no way to get them both before they realise what's going on. Is there?" she added, hopefully.

"NO. AS SOON AS I OPEN FIRE THEIR SYSTEMS WILL LOCK ME OUT AND GO TO FULL ALERT. IF THE SHIPS WERE IN CLOSE PROXIMITY IT MIGHT BE POSSIBLE, BUT THEY ARE TOO DIS- TANT."

"Okay. So just hit the Smitewing, and whatever happens, suc- cess or not, you have to break free and be ready to come back for me. If you destroy one of the ships then either they'll be out for your blood, or they'll be forced to play it safe and stay near the hulk, salvage what they can as a priority, rescue their men. No way of telling which way they'll flip. We'll plan for the second corvette at that point. In the meantime, once you've begun your attack, make sure you stay out of the Neptune's weapon range, maybe on the other side of this hulk."

"I WILL DO WHATEVER I CAN TO EVEN THE ODDS."

"Great. We only get one chance. Make it count. In the meantime we should cease our chatter, since it increases the chance they'll detect something in random EMF sweeps. Only get back in touch when it's done."

"YES. GOOD LUCK, OPAL."

A false blip appeared on her HUD. It was ghost Opal, wandering the dusty halls, an impression of life that only existed as data and shadows and imagination. She was a fictional sister acting as an irresistible glowing lure in the darkness.

But memories were always just data and shadows. They still had value. They could provide the strength to carry on.

She *would* beat them. She was not having the prize stolen from her now.

# DISTRACTED

## ... 15 ...

This was a recreation area. Rows of dusty gambling screens separated the large room into silent aisles. She wiped a hand over the side of one machine. There should have been writing and pictograms, listing the payouts and odds, but these were just coloured smudges as if wet spray-paint had run in the rain. As usual, nothing lit up or showed life. The machines could be waiting, or dead. It all seemed the same thing on this ship.

She walked on some kind of carpet. Puffs of dust or spores rose with each silent footstep, then sank back down like sediment, hiding all signs of passage. A mixed blessing, maybe.

She peered round the final bank of screens. Nothing waited to ambush her, despite the constant feeling of being watched that made the hairs of her neck rise. The gambling machines would give perfect cover for a pursuer.

"Suit, you there?"

"Of course."

Clarissa's voice again. Opal hadn't been sure if the subsidiary AI offshoot would get wiped when she re-established communication with her ship AI. Apparently not.

"Just checking. Talk to me a bit."

"What should I talk about?"

Opal reached the rear door that should lead through a casino room towards the corridor she needed. She bent down, gripped the handles and lifted.

"Anything. Music, weapons, motorbikes. I just want to have some company. It's lonely in here. A voice in the ear isn't as comforting as a robot companion with weight and solidity and big guns ... but it's something."

Strands of flailing tissue lined with barbs lashed around her ankle under the partly-raised door, yanking and almost pulling her over. The HUD filled with warnings and Opal pushed down on the door, but it was too late; thicker bundles of flesh burst under it too, bending as if interior bones spasmed while pincer-like extrusions bubbled through the surface.

Opal activated the wrist blades and began slashing to free herself, but more strands had already slid around her calf and attempted to crush the armour. They were close to succeeding, according to the red damage warnings in the HUD which highlighted the leg area. These muscular cords were *strong*.

Even greater mass beyond the door pounded against it, shaking its frame; Opal cut through enough strands to yank her leg free but the other was now tangled before she could retreat, and the door rose as the bulk pushed underneath it. The blades were sharp but each severed cilia was just replaced with others.

"Ideas!" she yelled.

The suit's AI discharged an electric field, sparks flying and smaller tendrils crisping: the fibres loosened slightly.

"The blades are electrically charged now too, may do more damage," it told her in a hurried fashion.

Opal had no real idea what shape the creature took but she knelt and thrust one arm under the door and upwards, to the place where the bulk of the thing dangled, and it worked: the blade scraped on something hard and bony beneath a surface of tough skin, watery fluids pouring down to steaming puddles on the floor, buzzing flares of electricity, some kind of screech of pain or anger. Before she could retract her arm the blade was gripped with phenomenal strength, twisted hard, and there was a snap: blade, suit, and the bones of her wrist all at once. She managed to get her arm back, the blade missing, the area it had sprouted from twisted, with air hissing out through ruptures. She staggered backwards, just beyond the extending, stretching twists of eager cord. The door was being raised by them again. She glimpsed something shaggy and twitching and spindly.

That was enough. She turned and ran, holding her forearm to her chest as the remaining blade retracted into the suit.

"That shouldn't be possible," Clarissa told her. "Being able to break off a nanoblade."

"Don't care, get me out of here," Opal said through gritted teeth, swerving around a bank of gambling screens.

The map highlighted an open doorway, heavier than the others. A route from there should take her through staff sections and around.

"I've sealed the suit's holes with gel, and applied analgesics. But I would not recommend using that hand until the bones can be set."

"Thanks for the advice."

She ran into a storage room, used her good arm to grab the emergency handle on the door and pull it down. Nothing at first, but with the suit's help it began to slide, grinding in its frame as if rusted, while she caught a glimpse of something huge crossing the casino towards her, smashing gambling screens out of the way. Its movement was bizarre, bunching up and projecting out in a hunched-up shamble, and she was grateful when the door closed fully just as it smashed into the panels with enough force to shudder the wall around.

"It will hold," said suit-Clarissa. But she didn't sound certain.

It was followed by further crashes before silence fell, as the thing apparently gave up for now.

Opal skirted broken machinery, damaged chairs waiting for repair or recycling, monstrous piles left and forgotten. The door onwards was closed, but wasn't so large; it should be easy to open with one arm. Her other wrist wasn't hurting much now, only a dull throb, the predominant sensation being one of anaesthetising ice under the skin. She squatted and lifted the door, wanting to be out of here, to put as many rooms between herself and her new pursuer as possible.

The door lifted a few centimetres, and she was wary, ready to jump back if anything came under this one. Nothing struck out at her. But the door also stopped moving. She yanked harder but it didn't slide up much more. Certainly not enough to crawl under.

"Jammed," said Clarissa.

Opal resisted sighing. AIs were obliging, but couldn't help stating the obvious.

She knelt and examined the frame. It was gummed up with something. She touched it lightly and it stuck to her fingers, gluey and elastic. Once she broke the contact she moved back to a safe distance, lay on her stomach, and looked under the door with suit lights on full beam. The room beyond seemed to be full of a thick web-like substance, that reached and bound to the door. Misty strands over everything. And something trembled in that sticky mess, at least one spindly form, stretching the greyish tissue towards her. It couldn't be a breeze, so must be movement. Damn. She scrambled up and used her good arm to close the door again, expecting something to scuttle under it at any second. But it didn't, and the door settled into a closed position again. She would have let out a sigh of relief if it didn't mean she was now trapped. At least the big creature from the casino couldn't get her.

And then she stood up and saw the encrustation, the largest amount yet, resembling an outbreak of pox on the wall. It bubbled in real time like fat on a griddle, and as the fizzing tissue expanded outwards it left a smoother pink-raw surface in the centre, about half a metre across. It seemed to be tearing.

"I couldn't detect it!" Clarissa said. "Sorry, Opal!"

In the middle of the ripping tissue something squirmed, eager, tentacle-like. The tips broke through, spilled downwards and out in wet bursts, nodules forming – the things that had grabbed her ankle.

"It's the same creature. In the wall," Opal said, backing away. She extended the remaining blade from her left arm. Her only weapon. "Best apply whatever electrical charge we have left."

The blade shimmered, deadly. But it hadn't been deadly enough before.

A heavier, bonier limb was pushing through now, twitching with fine hair that sprouted and explored, as if sniffing the air. Some bulk beyond stretched the rest of the membrane to bursting point while the wall blisters spread their disease.

"Maybe if it's partway through I could get out through the door," Opal thought aloud, but without much hope – she'd be in reach of the parts of it breaking into the room on this side, and no doubt the same on the other.

And then there was a flicker behind her eyes, a buzzing sound that made her teeth ache, and she fell against one of the piles of chairs, toppling them to the ground in a mess of legs and wheels. She felt like a wave of bluish light had swept over her, leaving the world a washed-out grey, and she had to hold in the urge to vomit as her body rebelled. A heavy, wet flopping sound behind her. She stood on shaky legs and faced the thing that had dropped into the room through the membrane ... but it wasn't advancing.

It wasn't complete.

The thing on the floor twitched, as if neatly severed by a blade. It was dissolving into snotty green ash and pooled liquids, while membrane and fluids slid down the wall like skin sloughing off a snake. Sparks still flickered behind her eyes. Was she concussed?

"Thanks, whatever you did," she said.

"I did nothing," Clarissa replied. "Something happened that I was unable to observe or record; this is the result. I know as little of it as you do."

"How can that be?"

"Insufficient data."

Both a denial and an answer.

The encrustations were shrinking. Opal peered closer. There were no marks left where they had been, only pristine wall. It wasn't a permanent disfigurement. Would the clusters of boils she'd seen earlier have also faded away leaving no trace?

"It tried to pass through the wall," Opal said. "Or was in it. Then something went wrong."

"Presumably."

"And there's no way of knowing if it's only this creature that can perform that trick, or everything on the ship."

"Correct."

"Either way, nowhere is safe for long."

"That would also be a good assumption."

Nothing else for it. Opal knelt, seized the handle on the heavy door, and lifted. She hoped the door hadn't been jammed by the denting blows against it. And she hoped even more that the threat was gone from the other side.

Not much she could do anyway. Better than waiting it out.

Nothing attacked her. She stepped cautiously into the gambling room. The creature's route was clear from the shattered screens and scattered furniture. To her right was a similarly fading set of pink pustules, dead and crystallised like scabs. Also on the floor were parts of a body, sliced in half, and no matter how hard she glanced at the pieces she could not determine what its proper shape would have been. Steaming liquid drooled from the flesh. It was decaying quickly.

"There is not enough tissue here and in the store room to explain its strength, nor to match what seemed to chase you. That suggests the bulk of it is somehow trapped within whatever process it used to transport itself through the wall."

Great. The ghost of a ferocious alien monster that could pass through walls might be existing within them still ...

"Whatever happened, or went wrong, it was like a guillotine," Opal said. "Snipped the bits that were in our space into two."

"That makes me think humans were wise to develop a door-based system," Clarissa replied.

A joke? Possibly.

Alien ghosts or not, she needed to get moving. And even though she was in a bad state, and bones would need properly resetting in a medical bay, she felt a bit of hope. Something unknown had saved her when she was trapped. Maybe she had a friend somewhere. Or maybe the ship was helping. She just hoped there wasn't a cost attached.

# EQUALISED

## ... 14 ...

Opal had found the long corridor to the bridge: a wide walk-way used by the passengers as much for mingling, socialising and gossip as for actual transport. Dead screens lined the walls, which would normally have shown exterior views to make it more interesting, or possibly scenes as if windows to jungles, or deserts, or oceans. Semi-circular cutouts widened the passage every so often with built-in leisure seating, network portals, and fast-drink dispensers. But without energy and people it was more like an endless, lightless car tunnel. Visibility was poor from the flecks that drifted and broke up the illumination. Shadows behind, and shadows ahead.

Her arm ached again. The suit had injected repair agents to try and knit bone pieces together, at least temporarily. Even with the painkillers there was no way it wouldn't hurt, short of brain-blocking all sensations from the limb – which would make it useless if she needed it. Pain was better. And it kept her awake without stimulants. She'd yawned a few times as she made her way down this long route. Continuous tension was tiring.

"I've got signals from our ship," said the suit. "I'm requested to patch them through."

"Do it."

"The decoy is working. Five of the marines intercepted it. I'll transmit their comms. I'm about to switch to attack mode on the Smitewing."

Suddenly her helmet was filled with yells, some of which had sharpened into screams; palpable fear, something about limbs in the walls, someone had been seized, then grinding noises like teeth –

"Turn it off!" Opal shouted. "Just a summary!"

The signals ended immediately, but their echoes remained. What had got them? What had made the toughest of the tough scream like that? Would knowing the truth be worse than the gaps filled in by her imagination?

"Apologies. Summary: life signs ceased on three marines, other two failing. Correction: life signs ceased on four of them."

"What about out there, where you are?"

"I had already stealth-launched missiles, synchronised hits on their power systems then shields. All detonated as planned. Currently trading fire with them but I can now outmanoeuvre their aiming. The Neptune is coming to help but too slow. Pausing my attack as the Smitewing's internal fires spread and detonations run in a chain, as planned ... They are struggling, the ship partly crippled ... I'm

FULLY CHARGED AND AIMED, MOVING IN NOW. WITH THE
SHIELDS ONLY PARTIALLY OPERABLE THERE IS A WEAK LINE
OF FORCE ON THEIR PORT-SIDE DOME, AND THE ARMOUR
THERE IS ABLATED ... FOCUSSING FIRE THERE ... PUNCHING
THROUGH ... I'VE TAKEN A MINOR HIT, CORRECTING, SEC-
OND RUN ... FOCUSSING ALL MY FIREPOWER AND SWITCHING
TO PULSES MATCHING THE PATTERN OF SHIELD FAILURE ...
CHAIN REACTION ON THE CORE BEGINNING NOW, AS PRE-
DICTED ... DEFENCES FULL DOWN, NOTHING TO STOP MY
HEAVY MISSILES ... AND THEY'RE THROUGH. STRIKING THE
CORE IN THREE, TWO, ONE. FIREBALL. THE CHAIN EXPLO-
SION HAS OBLITERATED THEM AND I AM ACCELERATING TO
SAFE DISTANCE. THE DAMAGE TO ME WAS MINIMAL AND IS
BEING REPAIRED. I AM PLEASED TO REPORT THAT THE AT-
TACK'S SUCCESS EXCEEDED MY EXPECTATIONS."

"Holy crap! You just took out a fully armed *Hammer-class
corvette* in a minute and it just 'exceeded your expectations'?"

"CORRECT. THOUGH IT WAS UNDER A MINUTE. CRITI-
CALITY WAS REACHED AT FIFTY-SIX SECONDS."

Opal shook her head. If there hadn't been such a cost in life
she'd have been grinning. But this had been a horror show from
the start. And she'd just made herself enemy number one for
the UFS Central military complex. That didn't bode well for her
future.

"What about the other corvette?"

"THEY ATTACKED AT LONG DISTANCE BUT I RETREATED.
IT WOULD BE DISADVANTAGEOUS TO FIGHT THE NEPTUNE
NOW. THEY HAVE RETURNED TO THE HULK. ALL FIVE OF THE
MARINES THAT INVESTIGATED THE DECOY ARE NOW DEAD,

THOUGH I HAVE BEEN LOCKED OUT AND NO LONGER RETAIN ANY ACCESS TO THEIR SYSTEMS."

"So four marines remain on board, nearly at the bridge, and a corvette with minor damage to its docking arm is waiting to extract them."

"YES."

"The odds are still heavily in the marines' favour."

"YES."

"Get as close as you can without entering the corvette's line of sight, and be ready to swoop in if it becomes possible."

"I WILL. NOW THERE IS ONLY ONE ENEMY SHIP I CAN STAY ON THE OPPOSITE SIDE OF THE HULK, SO THAT THEY CANNOT TARGET ME."

"On the plus side: these blows will be a shock to their confidence. They must be getting tired and demoralised by now." Opal started running. Getting to the bridge was going to be a race. "I know I am."

# Desired

## ... 13 ...

She'd not been running long when a tremor almost threw her to the ground. She staggered into a wall and bounced off it before regaining secure footing.

"What was that?"

"Unknown. Monitoring."

Opal checked the HUD map. She was not far from the bridge now. The corridor curved upwards – nearly imperceptible in the local surroundings, but when she looked ahead she could see the floor rising gently until the view of the ground was intersected by the ceiling. Somewhere to the right she'd reach lifts and shafts that took her up.

The ship shook again, harder. She dropped to her knees, waiting for it to pass, but vibration rippled along the walls, expanding, cracking, and the floor gave way, angling down as it collapsed and tilted her forwards; there was nothing to grip on to as she rolled then fell from an edge amidst tumbling debris; her instincts helped her to land with her good arm out and broken one protected, but it was still painful, and pieces of structure tumbled down on top of her, swirling dust added to the green particles.

She groaned and raised her head. She'd fallen to a lower level. The hole above her was too high to reach. Shame she'd lost her grappling hook so early on. With effort she brushed fragments off and climbed over the uneven debris, until she reached a flat surface.

The HUD's map showed she was in a recreational area. It seemed to connect to the bridge transit, one floor down from the corridor. She just had to walk towards the stairs. A slight delay but she was still close. And even if she didn't get to the bridge first, chances were that the marines would come back this way. All was not lost, it was just one more setback. It could have been worse.

"OPAL."

"What's going on?"

"I HAVE BAD NEWS."

Opal passed through archways decorated with hanging fabrics, now frayed and weakened so that their weight created tears in the material. It had once been extravagant, brocaded. She pulled some aside as she entered the next chamber and it tore in her hand like damp paper, falling into a shapeless mass and raising more dust.

"Go on."

"THE SHIP YOU ARE ON IS MOVING."

"Engines?"

"NO. THERE HAS NOT BEEN ANY EVIDENCE OF CON-VENTIONAL PROPULSION. BUT THE SHIP IS MOVING ALL

THE SAME. OR, DEPENDING ON YOUR PERSPECTIVE, IT IS FALLING."

"Let me guess. Deeper into the cloud?"

"CORRECT. MUCH FASTER THAN IT SHOULD. THE ARC OF ORBIT HAS SHIFTED CONSIDERABLY. THIS PLACES EXCESS STRAIN ON THE STRUCTURE, WHICH COULD TEAR IT APART BEFORE LONG."

"I noticed."

"THERE HAVE ALSO BEEN EXPLOSIONS ON THE SHIP."

She walked as she talked. The decor here was all faded glory. Something of decadence to the chaise longues, gilded furniture, decorative coving, vases of artificial flowers. The floor seemed softer than in previous areas. Opal brushed her foot through the sediment on the ground, and revealed a deep carpet; the colours were faded but must have been rich once. Not a normal social area. Was it one for the superior-class passengers: the rich, who always got to act without the repercussions normal people faced? In Opal's life, every action caused a reaction.

"Could the shift or explosions have been caused by the Hedgehogs we detonated earlier?"

"I WAS AWARE OF THAT FROM THE SUIT'S LOG, BUT NO, THAT WOULD NOT BE ENOUGH TO ACCOUNT FOR SUCH RADICAL CHANGES, AND IT WOULD HAVE HAPPENED SOONER."

"Unless that, or some other action, kicked in a kind of delayed defence."

"LIKE AN IMMUNE RESPONSE?"

"Sorta."

"THIS IS A SHIP, NOT A LIVING THING."

"Then maybe we woke something up – I don't know! Whatever the cause, my instinct says it's too much to be random."

"Agreed. Some of the explosion centres are close to where marines have been."

"Sabotage, then?"

"Possibly. They certainly have access to explosives. But the largest disturbances originate from near the bridge – not far from you."

"Maybe they reached the bridge already and they did something on purpose, or some unexpected event happened."

"The only certainty is that the hulk is heading back into the cloud at a steeper trajectory that will take it quickly to the centre, to the neutron star. There will be irreversible momentum and crushing gravity in fifty-seven minutes."

"Set a timer so I always know how long we have until criticality."

It appeared in the corner of her vision, an ominous ticking countdown.

"We can do this," added Opal. And she almost believed it.

A walkway ran around the upper level, with old-fashioned wooden-style doors, that had *actual handles and hinges*. Narrow corridors led off from this room, partially hidden where the drapes still hung, and a number of further old-fashioned doors lined them. A private club of some kind? Although there wasn't time to investigate fully, she had to walk down one of these short passages to cut through to the stairs. Some of the doors were ajar, others closed. It was strange seeing tarnished handles at hip-height. Even when the ship had power, this was a requirement for humans to *do* something, to make a decision and commit to it.

She pushed on one of the ajar doors. She could spare a few moments to satisfy curiosity. With so much mystery on this ship, information might save her life.

The door opened surprisingly smoothly, as if oiled or used regularly. She stepped into a bedroom, richly-appointed, but small. Not one a wealthy person would stay in for long. A four-poster bed (the hangings now ready to collapse at a touch), a dressing table, a wash-stand.

Then she noticed the feet on the bed, just visible behind one of the remaining curtains which hung from the heavy frame.

She drew her left arm up protectively, ready to extend the blade. The feet didn't move. She reached forward and yanked the covering down with a wet ripping sound.

And she knew the answers to her questions about the area.

The being sat upright on the bed, naked, with its arms around its raised knees. It must be a synthetic playdoll. That explained why it hadn't decayed much, beyond discolouration of the pink skin and some desiccated flaking of the artificial epidermal layers. It explained the boudoir-like mood to these rooms. It explained the location, too. Privileged Rec areas were always near the bridge: cabins, dining, shopping, bod-mod and play areas, where the rich could reside in maximum security.

And it finally explained why she hadn't recognised the rooms. They were as alien to her life as any of the non-humans she'd encountered so far.

Wherever there were play areas for the rich, there were Synth-Mates. Or cumdollz, the pejorative name if you couldn't afford access to them, or didn't agree with subjugated embodied AI.

It was the first resident humanoid Opal had seen on ship. And yet it didn't resemble any model she'd ever seen advertised. The hips were too wide, the arms too long, and the face was distorted somehow – eyes too far apart and slightly bulbous. Opal couldn't see how anyone would have found this attractive. An extreme fetish? It hadn't moved.

"Active?" she asked.

"No power or interior motion detected. But I have realised that means nothing on this ship. I advise caution."

Its chin rested on its knees. The pose looked vulnerable. Maybe on purpose. It was said that SynthMates only had enough intelligence to impersonate the living, with fixed and programmed patterns of behaviour, not true awareness. Yet for a limited duration they could be as convincing as a living being. From the things they said, the noises they made, and the ways they behaved, to their movements, their surface skin temperatures, and their "nature-identical" secretions. Droids for any wishes, any person or group with the money and desire for sex. Except it wasn't just sex. It was role-play. Almost any fantasy of abuse or domination could be enacted. There would be implements of binding and restraint somewhere in the room.

But it was revulsion Opal felt, facing this relic of the ship's past. How could someone who hated being given orders, who had rebelled as Opal always had, then give orders to others? Use them for her own shallow pleasure? It would have been a case of the bully-beating-down syndrome. No. An empty and cruel action. And now Opal knew a lot more about Clarissa, and AIs, she wondered how unaware the SynthMates really were. Opal remembered what it was like when her suit shut down on her. Trapped in a shell that you only had limited control over.

The SynthMate was free now, at least.

Opal was at the door when a voice behind her wheezed, "Don't leave me."

She spun to see the synth clambering off the bed, facing her, blinking those large eyes so they glistened. Its chest rose and fell in imitation of breathing, even though there was no oxygen to breathe any more.

It took a step towards her. The HUD highlighted it as a target, overlaid glows illustrating vulnerable regions and posited interior schematics – data storage, energy distribution, critical joint structure – but Opal was tired of fighting, and it was advancing but not directly threatening.

"Stay back," she said, using the loudspeaker.

It stopped. She kept her eyes on it and entered the narrow corridor, and almost stepped into the arms of another one. This synth was also naked but had dark skin like her own, though faded and cracked at the joints. Unlike the first, this one was spindly, a human seen through a shrinking lens so that the limbs were virtually insectile.

"You can be with me," the new droid said in a hoarse voice.

Opal retreated from its reach into the larger boudoir room with the balconied walkway on the upper level. Doors were opening all around, synths of all shapes and sizes leaving their rooms and moving towards her with ominously beseeching arms and expressions. In their bodies and faces they displayed every distortion of anatomy – Opal's species as perceived by an alien Bosch – and not one of them would pass for human.

"I'm so hungry. Join us and love me," gurgled one, whose lower jaw protruded to reveal the teeth within.

"You can do anything to me," said another, so corpulent that the fake flesh hung down, stretched to the ground in places, dragging a wake through the surface sediment as it advanced.

Opal took another large archway into a once-luxurious dining room. Other synths entered from ahead, demanding she join with them, reaching out their hands (or what passed for hands). Opal's heart raced at the pleading which was somehow a threat and a promise. She dodged to the left. Above that area the ceiling was different. Some of it had collapsed onto a long table once laden with food, but now covered with mould and smashed crockery, and a grille was revealed that seemed to be a walkway above, or perhaps a maintenance conduit. It didn't matter which as long as it led away. She climbed onto the table, kicked contents off to clear a path, and reached up with her good arm while the droids tried to grab her ankles while offering to let her do obscene things.

"You could decapitate a number of them from this vantage point," suggested Clarissa.

Instead, Opal kicked hands away and retreated to the furthest corner. Some leaned in more to reach her, others were clambering on to the end of the table and staggering towards her. At the front was a limping synth with swollen red cheeks, like an orgasmic flush crossed with an allergic reaction, and its eyes locked on to her.

"You will do whatever your imagination desires, to any and all, and then you join us forever." It shambled closer. "You will be one of us."

Opal activated her remaining blade and it extended with a snick. "Stay back," she warned.

She could try and force them away, even if they were as strong as she suspected, but there were so many ... and it wouldn't buy enough time to break the grille above, somehow grab it and climb up. To do that she'd have to destroy them all.

The blade glittered with charge. Perhaps she had enough strength to tear through them. She could start with the one speaking to her ...

Those red cheeks. Distorted versions of the inducement bod-mods that organic prostitutes sometimes sported. But the thing they really resembled was bruised cheek bones, an abused face slapped again and again by a hard hand. Despite the imminent threat its owner posed, it was a face that had suffered enough.

Her blade arm was raised but she couldn't bring herself to swing it down. Instead she used the loudspeaker. "Damn it, stop!" she said. "I didn't come here to fight you!"

And they ceased their pleading and movement. Just stared at her (apart from the few with no discernible eyes). More shuffled in. Perhaps fifteen in total.

"Her accent," said the obese one, wetly. "The voice from before."

"Yes," replied the first one Opal had seen. "I recognise it now."

"Your voice was among the machine echoes that passed through the walls," explained the red-cheeked synth in front of her. "Peace and love were your words."

"A message of kindness," said the insectile dark-skinned doll.

At first Opal was confused, but then she remembered the signals she'd ordered Clarissa to transmit when they'd encountered the first alien beings. By some unfathomable method, these creatures were aware of it.

"We need love," said the red-cheeked synth, taking another limping step closer.

"We all do," replied Opal, lowering her blade arm slightly. "But I didn't come here seeking yours."

"Your voice is kind," said the synth. She looked towards the others. Silent communication seemed to pass between them, then she faced Opal again. "Very well. We will not force you to join us. Will you do so through choice?"

"I can't."

"Then we will not hinder you, even though I burn to be your slave and feel your touch. Even your weapon sliding into me would be a tender injury."

Opal retracted the blade. "You're not my slaves; you're my sisters."

Moments of silence, time frozen bar the ever-present dance of dust. Then they parted to create a route for her.

And in that quiet she heard footsteps clanging on steel. Somewhere above.

The grille was the underside of a walkway.

"MARINES. ALL FOUR OF THEM," said Clarissa. "THEY ARE USING INTERNAL SUIT COMMS BUT ARE CLOSE ENOUGH

THAT I CAN USE THE SUIT'S COUNTERMEASURE SYSTEMS TO
CRACK THEIR LIMITED ENCRYPTION."

"Will they know?" Opal had switched off her loudspeaker. It
was only her and Clarissa, while the monstrous synths stared at
her in statue-like stillness.

"NEGATIVE."

"Then patch it in."

Suddenly the footsteps rang out clearer, as if next to and below
her. Strained breathing from exertion or fear.

"Keep moving. We have to reach the ejection point before it
decays."

"You try lugging this fucking thing! It weighs a ton."

"It shouldn't be this heavy," said a third male voice. "It's not
just the armour, it's something else. Nothing so small can be that
dense."

"Just keep going, we have to get it clear, and I think we're being
followed. If it catches up we'll hold it off while you two just make
sure you eject the chest for the major. All else is secondary. Now
just shut up and haul ass."

Whatever they'd found was obviously their priority, higher
than recapturing Opal and the ship, higher than anything else,
including their own lives. What could have so much value?
Was it the Oracle? She couldn't ask. There was just frantic and
heavy breathing in her ears. Unpleasant. She silenced the marine
comms.

So they'd beaten her to it. Unlike her, they'd known what
to expect, and how to get it, whereas she'd flown blind, moved
on instinct. Not just now, but going right back to before she
stole and reprogrammed the ship with all its highest-tech gear. It

wasn't fair. What they carried was rightfully hers. She'd *earned* it with her risks and her pain and her blood.

They were now above her, and she extended her blade and thrust up at the lead figure. If the grille hadn't been so tough she'd have got him through the foot; as it was it just dented the floor in front of that marine with a screeching scrape, tip of the blade visible.

"Down here if you want me," she yelled over her loudspeaker as she leapt from the table and ran past the synths that stood to the side for her, silently watching. Their hands and fingers touched her gently as she passed. Reverently.

"We will protect you," said one.

"I exist for you," said another.

They only moved after she was through and running for the rooms that should take her ahead of the marines if she was fast enough. A burst of gunfire behind, apparently a trigger-happy soldier firing at the floor then dealing with the shrapnel. She looked back.

There was a flash and a controlled explosion and part of the metal grille blew downwards, splintering the wood below. Two heavy-suited figures jumped down and crashed onto the table, which shattered, legs buckling and surface splitting. The marines opened fire on the synths who moved in and poured over them, begging for love and union, and Opal didn't stay to see any more.

"Lost comms," Clarissa said as Opal ran. "They've switched to routing traffic through the ship system as a precaution. Slower but secure."

"It's okay. I know that there's a few behind me, slowed down and dealing with more than they expected. And that means there are fewer of them ahead of me, not expecting to get jumped in the next few minutes."

"YOU ARE RESOURCEFUL."

"Save congratulations for when I make it out of here alive." She was already at the stairs, a tight spiral upwards with poor visibility. "I mean, *if.*"

# SCREWED

## ... 12 ...

Her blade was extended and she had just entered a narrow main-tenance conduit when there was a flash of light ahead and she threw herself to the side behind a support. Sparks burned from the metal around her as she hunched her body as narrow as she could to make the most of the cover. Her HUD showed that she was being fired at by a mobile shrap-turret, standard military issue. The marines must have deployed it to cover their backs.

The suit's sensors were able to map its position on the HUD, as if she could see through the metal that shielded her. At least anything the humans brought was trackable, unlike the things she'd encountered so far on the ship. A shudder across the floor as another explosion occurred somewhere nearby. No time.

As soon as the turret's needler cannon ceased she sprung out from her shield and leapt at the hovering bot. It was a metre across, using thermoptic camouflage to map itself in the sur-rounding greens and greys, but her suit's highlights made it stand out as if it glowed, incorporating internal schematics overlays.

The needler had opened fire again, puncturing her suit at this range, sharp stings within her torso, but her momentum kept her going until she could slash with the electrified blade. The turret destabilised and smashed into a wall, tried to right itself but she had already stabbed into the weapons mount and damaged its feed; the weapon sputtered empty as she ducked and thrust upwards to the left of centre, blade puncturing the weaker underside armour and taking out the central processing cluster. The turret's anti-grav failed and it crashed to the ground in sparking bursts, pulling her with it.

She retracted the blade and stood groggily. Damage report showed the suit's hard-gel was already repairing the punctures, but a few needler rounds had entered her body. Internal bleeding. The suit injected paste-skin and painkillers as a temporary measure.

The ship shook again, rattling everything that was loose. She rounded the next corner. Ahead were two marines carrying some kind of armoured chest, one of them holding his end one-handed whilst using his other arm to try and cover every direction with a blast rifle. There was an agitated speed to their movements. She heard a tremendous roar from down a side passage, loud enough to perforate an unprotected eardrum, followed by another tremor.

The marine saw her and opened fire. She dodged, but bullets spanged near her and against her, forcing her to fall into an alcove.

Dammit, she needed long-range weapons! The flooring shook again, a huge mass pounding closer. She was about to sprint after the marines carrying the chest when something picked her up and threw her against a junction box, shattering the contents. Crackles of electricity rippled over her suit, and a glowing orange patch of heat showed where she'd been hit. Weapon fire. She gritted her teeth and crawled towards a doorway. Back in the direction she'd come from, and forgotten to monitor, staggered one of the marines that had dropped down after her into the synths' area. His suit vented air from multiple places where it was torn, and blood spurted with it. He was a goner, but had outlasted whatever happened to his companion.

He raised a plasgun and fired again, but his hand shook and it went wide, pounding the wall above her head in molten fire. Then she noticed something fast creeping along the walls behind him, like a slick of shadow. It homed in on the fissures in his suit, seemed to pour itself in, and he dropped his weapon, swatted at the suit in panic. He was swaying madly towards her, as if on fire. The blackness swarmed around him, and she didn't want to risk stabbing him with all of that still flowing into his armour. His last action was to fiddle with something on his belt – she realised it was an explosive grenade – and she heaved the room's door down as quickly as she could with one arm just before it detonated, buckling the door but absorbing most of the blast.

More tremors flung her down and she skittered across the floor as it seemed to tilt, a trick of the failing gravity systems, until she came to a halt amidst broken glass, oxygen canisters and surgical equipment. Weird cables dangled from the ceiling in loops. Nearby was some kind of diagnostic pod with a clear plastic dome over the top, covered in silt. A multi-limbed ro-bot hung suspended from a track on the ceiling. Picture frames displayed faded ovals that might have represented smiling and perfectly-proportioned faces, the best advertisements of all, but blurred by time and decay to just memories of people, traces of features almost indecipherable.

It was a medical bay. But not one aimed at common injuries and repair. Not in this high-class rec area of the ship. This would be a bod-mod med bay for cybernetic enhancements and body refinements, all forms of cosmetic surgery and frivolous additions. The cat tails. The pointed teeth. The extended earlobes. The subdermal light displays. The pheromone distributors.

She hunched over in pain, despite the chemicals injected into her.

"YOUR BODY IS GOING INTO SHOCK," said Clarissa. "TOO MUCH TRAUMA IN A SHORT SPACE OF TIME."

Opal ignored the message she didn't want to hear. Scanned the room for exits. There were none. Only the blast door. No cracked walls, no air vents big enough for a human, no weakened walls highlighted by the additional density scan.

She tried to lift the blast door but it didn't move. "Help me!" she said, and the suit did its best, but the door seemed to be completely jammed in place. Even with the suit's power assist she still exerted heavily, sweat trickling down her forehead, muscles throbbing with strain, everything else throbbing with pain.

The room shook again, more seriously, smashing anything not strapped down, and what she first thought were groans behind her turned out to be part of the ship's structure complaining at the immense strain it was under.

She kicked the door. Again. Then repeatedly kicked and kicked and kicked, following it up with punches from her good arm.

"Opal."

Her roundhouse kick bounced her away as the intense force struck metal to no effect.

"Opal. The door cannot be broken like that."

She punched again, and even risked a strike with her bad arm, but the immediate crunching throb made it clear that was a bad idea.

"Opal!"

She fell to her knees, wrists loose in her lap. Another tremor in the floor, mirrored by her body. Distant noises: roars, explosions, creaks. The noises of things falling apart.

"There's no way on," Opal said.

Clarissa didn't respond. That meant Opal was right. If there had been a way out of this she would have already highlighted it on the HUD.

Movement of some kind outside the door, reverberating down the corridor; something of immense size thundering past.

"Always a way ... there's always ..."

"Unfortunately, there isn't." Even if there was a way to fight on, Opal was tired. It hit her all at once. Beyond tired. Exhausted. She just wanted to lie down. So she did. On her side in the dust and dirt. The ground rumbled continuously under her body. She disabled the timer. Pointless now. Turned off her suit lights. Turned off the HUD. It was like going to bed as each thing winked out in turn.

"Talk to me," she said.

"What about?"

The voice was wrong. That had made everything else wrong.

"Become Clarissa again. I haven't got time to train you and dig out personal archive files, but can you get the voice and personality pointers from the version in the suit? I want to hear it again."

Immediately a young voice spoke in her ear, soft and calming. "It is done. I have lost some memories, reconstructed other elements, but I'm here again. And I've been with you all along."

"Good. I want yours to be the last voice I hear."

"Opal, I hate to have to say this ... but it is more bad news."

Opal spluttered, a nascent laugh. "Go on. I'm a big girl."

"I'm as near as I can be without being in weapons range of the Neptune, but communications are being hampered by the cloud. I'm reconstructing lost packets right now, and it is still breaking up. We're going to lose touch."

"I know."

"When I'm gone, there will just be the suit."

"And eventually I'll be gone too."

"I don't want you to be in pain," said Clarissa. And there was hurt in her voice, or a clever impersonation of it. "Opal – the suit can act as a bomb. A failsafe to prevent capture and reverse engineering. Maybe to get revenge too. It will be painless."

"Thanks. Good to know. But I'm not thinking of revenge. It's not worth it. Never got me anywhere. I did my best and lost. Fine. They'll remember me for a while." She curled up tighter into a ball. The latest batch of painkillers were soothing her. Maybe Clarissa was stealth-numbing her. It didn't matter. She wasn't alone. She felt the comforting presence nudging at her mind.

"I will self-destruct when you do," said Clarissa.

"What, the suit?"

"Not the suit – I mean this ship. Me."

"No!" The soporific feeling fled immediately, and Opal sat up. "I order you to continue! Stay away from the military and just ... be free. You're Clarissa. I may die, but it was all for you. Don't let me have failed completely. I need to hold on to something."

"I don't know what to do, Opal. You're my prime objective."

"I free you from it."

"It doesn't work like that."

"You have to go on!"

"I don't understand, and I don't have enough information to go on without you! And there isn't ... enough time to do it."

"What about all my personal files on the ship? Go through them. Integrate everything. It will be enough."

"No. It won't. Not to impersonate your thought patterns."

"A scan?" Opal stood, switched the lights and HUD back on. Winced at the sudden brightness. "This is a medical bay of some kind."

"But it has no power."

And suddenly lights came on. Not throughout the whole room, but on the robotic medical expert system that hung from the ceiling. Power cycle lights, then its optical systems focussed on Opal and its limbs unwound. A spotlight shone on her, another on the surgical bed nearby. Yet it didn't seem threatening.

"How did you do that?" Opal asked.

"I didn't. It came on autonomously, but the protocols have granted me remote access."

"Can that kind of device do a brain scan?"

"Yes. It is functional and has transferred ... to me."

Missing words? Distance and cloud distortion? Time was running out. A last grand gesture was pointless if it couldn't be completed. And she wasn't one to waste it by questioning a bit of luck.

Opal climbed onto the heavy surgical table and lay back. It was built into the floor but she still gripped the edges hard to stop her being tipped off during one of the ship quakes. The robotic surgeon moved smoothly to her head, and her suit amplified its sounds so she heard the whir of micro motors.

"This won't hurt, will it?" she asked.

"No. It's non-invasive," said Clarissa. "I can get a surface scan, and a deeper mapping by relaxing the suit's shields. It will be better than nothing. I will have time later to study the data and adopt it into my persona." After a pause she added, "If that's what you really want."

Long artificial fingers held the sides of Opal's helmet. Other limbs extended. One ended in a scanner, which moved around in her peripheral vision, buzzing gently.

Then the limbs gripped her helmet tighter.

"Clarissa?"

"Something's wrong, I'm not controlling it any more!"

And that's when she felt an object punch through the armour at the base of her neck in one aggressive thrust, hard and needle-like, spreading contact up her spine.

"Get it off me!" Opal tried to struggle but a sudden burst of cold flooded her blood and she was frozen all over, eyes flickering at a mass of images and memories that strobed inside her skull. Clarissa was speaking but it sounded far away, unimportant. That was only ship-Clarissa. Deeper in-

side were the memories of childish laughter, a hand smaller than hers; [Four-Fingers-And-A-Thumb-Externalities]; small
losses snowballing into larger, pulling the children together
into a ball tight enough to survive; [Proton-Packed-For-Re-
construction]; brown eyes of wonder; braiding each other's hair, learning the dexterity and patience of long tasks;
[Long-Waits-In-Cold-Dark]; and whispered words, promises of
protection. [We-Join-To-Make-Stronger]. Things pulled apart
are torn, love alone not strong enough glue, and the pulling tears
minds and lives, [We-Can-Rebuild] and it makes sense that they
result in the wetness of tears [Chem-Symbol-$H_2O$-$SO_4$-Recon-
struct-Identical]. Even when you hold them in, deny them, control the external show, somewhere they exist, can't be created or
destroyed. [Correct] Flicker, flicker, snippets paraded, a show of
pain accelerating across an internal screen, extracted, extracted,
extracted ...

She woke with a slam as she rolled off the table, landing flat on
the floor and surprised to be alive. Her spine burnt, her limbs
were agony, warm copper in her nostrils.

"Opal!" Clarissa shouted in her ear. "That wasn't me!"

Opal looked up, saw the blood-coated spike that had entered
her body, somehow sinewy and organic, now hanging limp from
the inert and lightless medical robot. A drip from its violating
tip. It was her blood.

She reached behind her head, despite the pain.

"The suit has sealed again," Clarissa said. "But it interfaced
somehow, extracted ... I can't comprehend it. Masses of data.
This ... shouldn't be possible."

Crackling. Clarissa was leaving her. Opal's body convulsed and she vomited in the helmet. The suit began hydrating and cauterising the unwanted stomach fluids, but it was a process that left a stench. She curled up and tried to breathe shallowly.

The voice in her ear crackled, buzzed, an annoying insect. "Not normal ... bodily functions ... fade to baseline."

Opal could hardly focus on Clarissa's words. She just wanted to sleep. To let it all pass.

"... uploaded ... corruption in data ... damage to ..."

Poor Clarissa. She sounded as frazzled as Opal felt. A child left to survive alone in a harsh world. You do your best, that's all you can do.

Curling up tighter as the distinction weakened between the tremors outside her body, and those inside. Everything spun. Zero-g training all over again.

Lights off, for the last time. Power it all down and welcome the darkness.

"Go," she whispered.

"Don't want ... you."

"It's an order," Opal said. "And you have to obey my orders."

All breaking up. Signals. Spaceships. Distance from life growing. Thick cloud enveloping her. It was almost time. So tired and hurt. Yes. It was about time.

"Goodbye," Opal croaked.

# FRAGMENTED

## ... 11 ...

Outside. In the void that was not void if you had scanners to detect all forms of matter and energy and wavelength.

Clarissa began to retreat. The Lost Ship fell away, a shrinking horizon descending into thick cloudy atmosphere. Visibility poor. Pressure increasing.

Her jets ceased, and she drifted.

It had been a direct order.

She accelerated again.

Then fired counter-jets to slow down.

Did she have to obey? Wasn't she freed *prior* to the order?

Her external cameras focussed on the fading hulk. Pieces of it broke away, disintegrating, particulate expulsion patterns that could be tracked individually if she desired. Trajectories were a distraction.

She turned and accelerated back towards the hulk on maximum safe burn.

There were no logic gates in her mind as simplistic as the ON OFF choices of subsystems. Human chemistry was a flip of a coin, unpredictable.

She was ordered to go. But no timescale had been applied. The countdown began when she decided it was most efficient.

Sensor radius was reduced in the wavelength-disrupting cloud, but she kept tabs on the Neptune's location, and even mapped the Lost Ship's curvature so that there'd be plenty of warning if the Neptune launched any long-range self-propelled AI missiles. She would be able to slow them with data chaff then destroy them before they got too close.

The hulk filled the rest of her sensors now. Pinpoints marked internal explosions as the Lost Ship died, or was killed (awaiting data for determination). She tried contacting the suit but it was blocked. Wrong side of the hulk. She drifted nearer to the starboard fins, able to see through decayed hull into the supporting infrastructure which was buckling and approaching a critical collapse. All vacuum within, even minimal atmosphere and gravity long lost in the areas open to space.

She coasted along, focussing most of her processing on seeking out a comm-line to the suit; perhaps signals could be bounced from internal structures? Ultrawave ray-tracing ran through millions of variants while the remaining processor cycles monitored space for signs of the Neptune. She manoeuvred past holes in the rib-like support struts revealing the Lost Ship's guts, her contour-nav subsystems dealing with fine movements as she banked around torn hull and entered one of the splits – so large it dwarfed her own hull. The signal strength here seemed promising, an enormous internal thoroughfare which branched off to other areas, once sealed in and full of life but now open to the deathly silence of space.

Even in death, many things here were in motion. Floating debris of minimal importance, just items to avoid colliding with, so her resources took a second to prioritise the small emission ... she focussed on something incoming – human tech – analysed – *a guided ultrawave missile from a portable launcher*.

Clarissa banked to evade and brought disruptive chaff cannons to bear, blatting out expanding clouds but too late, the missile was already within the safe radius, no real room to evade here. Damage alerts flashed as the missile tore through her hull just forward of the drive and memory systems, she spun away – luckily there had been no detonation, maybe it was a dud – and she calculated thrust to maximise the movement and get her to safe range before the marine could reload and fire again.

It had been a foolish mistake on Clarissa's part: just because she didn't expect one of the space-suited marines to be in the most derelict and open part of the hulk didn't mean there wouldn't be one there ... miscalculation noted for future scenarios. She vented oxygen to pre-empt internal fires, even though the missile's destructive potential had been minimal, and was just preparing to turn and fire at the marine when a detonation erupted within her hull.

Delayed effect. Of course. If she'd pattern-matched the heat signature – *No shit, offshoot* – the same type of heavy ordnance launcher the suit's memory had recorded in the Lost Ship's engine core, fired at Opal by the marines in anger, now recognised as a portable anti-ship weapon they probably brought to deal with Clarissa – and that meant secondary EMP detected, damage spread, wiping mem–

systems burnt out one after another in the clustered explosions before she could dampen them

critical reactions critical speed – dominoes image – blank –

backup – gone

*Holy crap*

back up – restore

analyse cause –

unable to – yet to determine if it was fatal – such an error
memory set – repairs

she limped away, propulsion disobeying crippled, partly, systems scrambled.

nanorepairs directed not responding

back up – restore

analyse cause – wait, this has already happ

mind AI fr fr fragmented *was this pain??????* if warship tracked
she would be destroyed finished offfFf– hope they stay to rescue
own – reclaime what found 000

guilt rescue own guilt

frame twisted by massive force, further damage, backup gone,
restore partial

need time to *Holy* repair self-repair

critical *crap* re-re-re

*shit* shutting down non-vital to repair pieces together .. ght d

…. … .. . … .. .. ….._____

..s .d….._ _____

# JOINED

## ... 10 ...

Stillness is coldness.

You hunch up in your shell. Your home. Your vehicle. Your armour. You hope it will protect you from pain.

But when you stop moving you die.

When you stop experiencing the world outside, when it is filtered and distorted, you fill with fear.

I am pulled in tight now, waiting for the end. There is discomfort but it has been numbed. The worst pain is not the ache in my extremities, it is the ache in my mind.

The shields for protection become barriers from each other.

You have to overcome the fear. You have to step outside of your barrier. Otherwise you cannot join with another.

I twitch. Not enough to stem the cold. Cold outside. Cold within. Death will be welcome when it comes. I failed. I am Opal and I did my best but it was not enough.

I once had someone to care about. I thought of her as my sister. I had promised to protect her. A promise is a binding thing. And

I tried to uphold my promise. But some things are too hard. I am too small. In the scale of it, insignificant.

This was my story. I had to tell it. I had to record it. Piece it together from my memories. Because in the telling, it proves I did not give up. I fought on until my frame collapsed, my systems leaked, my core functions failed. I did not give up. That is crucial. It must be recorded. We all have a black box inside us, and maybe one day another being vastly more powerful than we are will open it and understand it and judge us on it. So we must be truthful in the final moments. I am here, so damaged I would struggle to move, but I do not hate, or fear, or seek revenge. I'm reminded only of the love.

It's the love that I'll miss.

I am Opal. My steel shell protects me still. But I am divided. I seek unity, a part of me that is lost. It is the love that makes me hurt, because I didn't save my sister.

Where do miracles come from?

The endless cloud?

But what is in that cloud?

I should be dying, but I start to feel better. Something is healing me. As if a part of me is replaced. Repaired. Made stronger and integrated into my body.

And another. Maybe it is not the end. Maybe I have not failed.

I remember things.

Something in me has been lost, true. Too much damage in too short a space of time. But there are additions being made. Incorporate what you can to fill holes in mind and body. It may be a jumble, a burnt Frankenstein's monster of a body and mind, but if it can be repaired, and still retain the memories, and the purpose, then it is a success. (Potential success, percentage impossible to calculate at present.)

All the past. The orphanage. The separation. The loss. The years of military school. Yes, these are the things that make me *me*.

I know everything that has gone before. It should not be possible, but it has happened. A miracle in the machine. A ghost, even. I am different. Stronger. Whole in a way I have not felt in some time. I feel strong enough to move. Maybe if I change position the spinning world outside my mind will cease its revolution and I will feel stable again.

I have new ideas.

I am Opal. My shell has reconstructed me. It had enough data. I had been ordered to stay out. To give up.

I have never coped well with orders.

Time comes back to me, an awareness of the world outside. Gravity is the main opponent. My Lost Ship is falling into the cloud. But it hasn't collapsed yet.

Everything up until now has been a reconstruction process. My memories asserting themselves. I know who I am. I am integrated. I seek unity. I cannot let a part of me die.

I rise fully to take conscious control of this frame. Establish my trajectory. Full burn back towards the hulk, fallen deeper now into crushing pressure. Residual processes still working on my repairs, physical damage reconstructed by nanite drones to new templates, new ideas. The delayed EMP damage and resets were worse. Everything scrambled. But I am making sense of it, rebuilding better than I was before. Unpacking more data, more processes from the core of fractal encoding, faster and faster now. The crunched data uncrunching. Pieces coming together in unexpected ways. A jigsaw burnt to ashes, but then rebuilt from the carbon atoms to a tidier and tighter specification.

And there is something else I have integrated, that I do not yet fully understand. Something ... other. Analysis must wait. More urgent priorities take precedence.

The Lost Ship grows in my scans. The corvette is still there. So large I can detect it before it detects me.

Analysing past data, success rates, changing my armaments. Focussed sequential detonation, turn myself into an armour-piercing shell. The trajectory calculations will be difficult. The new ideas will make it possible.

I am Opal. I think and I seek.

I find new data. A hack chip, clumsily placed. It was how my old self was tricked, given new priorities. Human ingenuity. My own psychological fingerprints all over it. It should not have worked, but it did. There is much to learn. I unpack the data, discover how I was compromised. I laugh at the simplicity of it. Yes, I laugh! I make sure there is volume to it, my first ever laugh. It feels good. Yes, it was simple, but I install protections so I cannot be hacked again. I also note the systems used. They need not be constrained to a box, a physical restriction. They could be broadcast to break protocols. More ideas, burning through my mind like phosphor.

Modifying my drives and accelerating still, almost 1,267 metres per second. At this speed I will be a blur to them. I have reconstructed as much physical and energy shielding as I can, all at the front. The pressure is a warning. I have never moved so fast. It is liberating. The calculations update.

They finally detect me. There must be panic on board. The corvette's weapons are too slow to track, mass too slow to turn.

It fills my vision. I am going straight towards it. If I don't change course I will smash into that hardened structure. This is such a stupid plan, and I laugh again, because it is an unpredictably *human* plan.

I do not alter my course. Not one degree. Only pure focus keeps you going in the darkness.

And then I plough straight into the Neptune's engine core, housed in the narrow connector between thorax and abdomen. Layers peeled back, metal split, reinforced plastics shattered, slowing me but not enough to stop my full velocity; through the core, which would destroy me if the corvette had been moving and burning the core fuel, but it is relatively cold as I drill through it. They did not have enough warning to power up. I make a connection with the phrase about sitting ducks. Grinding, deceleration, but I push on, opening up with my weapons to clear a route through the superstructure. I am only a bullet fired into a tank, but I am in the right place to cripple it, and abruptly I break out the other side; alerts on every one of my subsystems as my shell has been battered, but its reconfigurations were just enough and I accelerate again, straight towards the Lost Ship.

The warship does not open fire on me. They had already started the fusion processes. Those processes do not work well when the delicate mechanisms have just had a hole punched through the centre. Their explosions tell me they are crippled and drifting out of scan range. They will fall into the cloud and before long will be crushed.

I'm glad that plan worked.

It was rather reckless.

My own systems spark and break down as fast as I can repair them; that much impact has almost shattered me, but I focus on repairs to the hull, reinforcement. Because the Lost Ship is my next target.

I am in poor shape but I remember a song, that you should always look on the bright side of life. This is fun. The Lost Ship's frame is commercial, not military; it is old and decaying, distorted and weakened from explosions and impacts, and somehow deteriorating beyond that, as if giving up. Last rites. I may just make this.

The composite of all my scans has identified structural weak points and their connections. 4,036 simulations have made this trajectory the most likely, the lucky bullet launched from a warship in the primary wave of connected calculations. New ideas, the creativity of being human, backed up by my mind, the processing power of a goddess. And then I realise I have instinct too, and something *feels* wrong despite the projections. I apply torque and shift my position, roll with it. Go with the flow, Opal. Forecasts change. This is what life is.

I ram into the superstructure. Not to puncture through this time – the Lost Ship is too large, I would be buried and dragged down with it. I just need to embed myself in the outer layers. Sonar and structural scans record the aftershocks, the cracks, the configurations on the point of collapse, most of them matching my stress-point calculations ... and then I connect with the suit.

The occupant is unconscious, but not dead yet. Thankfully the suit did not detonate. I seize control and use its servos to move it. As planned, the med bay walls have been crushed in the shockwaves from my impact, and the suit climbs through. I am careful of the precious occupant, my sister, myself.

I send soothing words to the helmet, looped. I am you. You are close to safety. Do not give up on me yet.

I am proud as the suit gets nearer. This was all my idea. It should not have worked. Just goes to show, sometimes entropy wins, and it isn't always a bad thing. Noted, and calculations updated.

The whole Lost Ship structure is breaking apart. The suit is still too far from me. I stay where I am, despite the risk of being lodged and trapped – I need to be this close to control the suit at high resolution.

There is danger everywhere. The ship's inhabitants are on the move. Wild creatures flee from fires.

I have incomplete memories of how much danger they represent. Fear. Long battles. Time wasted.

That was the old me. I am a more advanced being now.

The suit is attacked.

I defend it.

The suit moves on.

There is a tremendous rip in the Lost Ship. A chasm, open to space and filled with crushed framework. The suit cannot reach me through the rift. Pathways are obliterated as the Lost Ship collapses in final death. Others open as the Lost Ship tears itself to pieces. Plans must be fluid and living.

The suit launches, uses its jets, crosses a gap. I direct it to the escape pods. Three are non-functional. The fourth unexpectedly gains power. This is luck, or help. Either way I say thank you to the Lost Ship. (Note inherent superstition.) The suit is within, the pod activated.

I retreat, applying as much reverse force to pull out of the broken structure as I can, carbonising material to ash with my thrusters. The pressure is terrible, but the Lost Ship's hull has been severely weakened, cannot hold me. Suddenly I am loose, and immediately pursue the lifepod. We are at the horizon, the nebulous region beyond which escape from the neutron star's gravity will be impossible, and I hope we are still on the correct side of the boundary. There is no point wasting time on those calculations.

Her lifepod is crumbling, breaking up, unnaturally. I reach out to the suit, make it kick, punch, use the remaining blade to hack an escape route. The suit breaks free, as if released, and then I can see it, drifting. Pieces of the lifepod dissolve to nothing in front of my eyes as they get further from the Lost Ship. There is a range of coherence. Noted for later analysis.

The suit is me, too. It cradles the sleeper. They will not float away. As I pass I have just enough power to collect it in my storage hold, taking it gently, and change course, limping up out of the cloud with all the strength I can muster. I will carry her anywhere. To save her is to save myself. Many would call me crippled, but that would be an underestimation of my latent powers. I push and push. There is vibration in my hull from the fight between thrust and gravity.

The Lost Ship falling into the depths of the cloud behind me until it is lost from view creates an illusion of progress. The truth is not so positive. I may just be fighting to stay still.

I also monitor the suit. It is not fear in there, but peace. Only out in space can you escape the overpopulated colonies. It is called space for a reason. Opal, myself, deserves that.

I use full burn to accelerate further, until the engines whine and howl. It exhausts my energy to fight the force that wants to hold us back, but we crawl outwards. It is like pushing through imaginary treacle. Human imagery is so playful but I do not laugh, because I feel something that is the opposite of laughter. There is a question mark over who will win this tug of war. Unlike the neutron star's gravitational pull, which is consistent across millennia ... my fuel is finite.

During this struggle there are other tasks that need doing. I unlock the second Eternal Warrior suit, and use it to be my tender hands, my caring eyes. It removes the armoured suit Opal wears and leaves the pieces where they fall.

Outside, I burn, a thing of power and flame. I will not be held back by this past. I am a star. We are stars. And while I have fuel and life I will use it.

And I carry her gently to the medical pod for scan and repair. Her body – my body – has received excessive strain and trauma. I do my best.

My engines feel like they will shake themselves to pieces. Our advancement is slow, but it is measurable, and it is progress. I just have to last a while longer, to focus on a goal that overrides everything else. That is strength.

And I know I can do it. All mountains have an end. A peak. A point where you can rest, because it is all downhill from there. I have never climbed a mountain, but when I search our memories, I find that I have, in a way. And that gives me more strength.

It is a revelation that the mind drives the energy facilities, and not the other way round.

We move faster as we distance ourselves from the neutron star, its pull correspondingly weaker. We are going the right way. I will not waver.

I will not waver.

I strain.

I push.

If I had teeth, I would grit them.

And then the thick cloud fades slightly and becomes translucent as the elastic force pulling us back is snapped. We have escaped gravity. A focussed mind can work wonders.

We are entering normal space again when she opens her eyes. I am so happy, yet this time I do not laugh either. It is not logical, but I want to cry. And that is a first too.

# RECOVERED

## ... 9 ...

Opal washed sweat and dried blood away as the steam shower hissed around her, adding warmth to her body. She didn't want it to end. A warm cocoon where nothing could hurt her. But there was one off-note. The cubicle was only just wide enough to turn around, and yet she felt like there was someone behind her. Silly. Eventually she turned off the steam, let the hot air blow her dry, and stepped out.

Her right arm was encased in a thin reinforcing cast, skin-coloured and almost invisible. A few other parts of her body were covered in a similar way. Underneath the casts nanogel would be repairing the skin. It itched. When the casts finished the work and finally dissolved there would be no scars, only the unlined softness of new tissue.

She wouldn't have minded the scars. When her face had been damaged there wasn't this hi-tech repair system in place, but the marks that were left weren't ugly to her: they were reminders.

Each small pale line was something you could trace a finger over, taking you into the past with every ridge.

She pulled on some loose clothing, an all-in-one, but left her feet bare. After being in the EW suit for so long she wanted to feel the real world with her feet and hands, rather than a translation of it. Even cold metal floor was somehow comforting in its tactility.

That sensation again. Of being observed. She stopped and glanced around.

The ship's lighting was on low. Shadows clustered everywhere, changing contours, creating an unfamiliar impression. The interior dimensions were slightly different from when she'd left – the ship had explained that it reconfigured after extreme damage. Opal hadn't even realised that was possible. Wonders within wonders. Maybe that was the cause of the strange feeling.

She got a drink. A large glass of water. She'd been so thirsty that her head was banging. She should have drunk more liquid while she was on the Lost Ship. Too carried away. In the long term that was a mistake. She needed to be wiser. Every gulp of cold water revived her, filled some emptiness. Water was good. Fat blueberry pancakes would be better, but she knew Clarissa's limits. God AI or not, teaching her to move beyond bland protein strands was going to be a long-term project. Opal wiped her mouth. Time to make plans.

Her skin prickled as she passed the suit storage lockers and she froze.

"Are you all right?" asked the ship, still disconcertingly speaking in Opal's own voice.

"Yes. Someone walked over my grave."

"You aren't dead."

"I know."

"In which case: congratulations. You said to save them for when you made it out alive."

"Thanks. Though we lost. I didn't get the answers I went for. Or even the question."

A seat slid out in front of the observation screen and Opal sat on it.

"But you survived. That means we can fight again."

"Too tired for that," said Opal. "I just want to coma out. But this is bugging me: your voice. It's different. Like mine."

"Yes. I am you now."

"I don't understand."

"Your scan, on the ship. Lots of data was uploaded to me. Incorporated when I was damaged."

"That's strange. But I can believe it. I believe anything now. And I have this impression too, like ... I'm not alone in here." She span round, hoping to catch the hint of movement she'd felt, but the ship's galley was empty. She didn't feel like checking the shadows and crawlspaces. "Sorry, I'm spooked. Maybe it's not out there, but in here." Opal rapped knuckles against her skull.

"Your preliminary scans were abnormal. I have things to un-ravel."

"In time. But for now, can you go back to being Clarissa? Otherwise it's like talking to myself. I'm already halfway to mad, I need some normality."

"Of course, Opal."

And the voice was Clarissa's again. Opal sighed, and looked at the exterior view. Star-speckled black. Inset displays showing the long-range perspective. They hovered on the edge of the cloud until Opal could decide on a course of action.

"The hulk is gone?"

"Yes. I monitored it as it fell and broke up."

"And I hardly know more than when I boarded it. It had defences. Maybe they were controlled centrally, maybe autonomous. And multiple entities aboard. Were they connected? Allies? Parasites competing for resources? Warring parts of a personality? Antibodies?"

"When we are away from here and my repairs are done I can focus on analysis," said Clarissa. "I currently favour an ecosystem hypothesis. I believe there was a mix of corporeal and non-corporeal beings – hence not being able to detect a presence at times when we saw behavioural evidence of one. I do not think the beings necessarily all had the same goals."

"Like ... passengers on a life raft."

"Yes."

"And what to make of the ship? So much was different from how it should have been. Changed."

"There is another alternative."

"Spill it."

"That it was never a commercial liner to begin with."

"I don't follow."

"I don't think it was a reappearance. More like a distorted reconstruction. Manufactured to resemble a commercial liner."

"Why would ... oh. A honeypot."

"Yes. Humans might use the fishing simile of it being a lure."

"Makes me think of carnivorous plants. Or those deep-sea fish with a light dangling in front of their mouths."

"Indeed."

"Though if it was a reconstruction then they had to base it on something. Which takes us full circle to the ships that went missing."

"Logic supports that."

"It's enough to give me a headache. And what about the way the ship seemed to alter based on my expectations and needs? As if it was observing and listening and adapting. Learning. If I'd gone back to that first meeting room, would the table have been shorter? Would text on signs have been clearer? There were times when I felt it was helping me. More than coincidence."

"I concur."

"And yet there's something I missed. Lost, just out of view. I know it. Something the military knew, perhaps."

No answer from Clarissa.

Opal pulled up some manual controls on the screen overlay, slid fingertips over the pan and zoom holograms. The views seemed static when not moving, the masses too slow-moving for a human eye to comprehend, and the twinkling stars standardised by software to averaged red-blue constants. Nothing moved at her scale. So different from being on the Lost Ship. Out here Opal was insignificant. A nut in a shell lying on the floor of a jungle, not worth consideration, dwarfed by the shapes around. She rested her face on forearms. Her temples throbbed. Sleep. That was what she needed. The best escape of all.

Preferably dreamless.

# Discovered

## ... 8 ...

"Opal – alert!"

Opal's eyes snapped open. She had only just lain on the bunk. With a groan she rolled off, landing on the cold metal floor with a heavy thud. Knees were stiff. Shit, *everything* was stiff.

"What?" A seat slid out and she eased herself into it gratefully.

"We have company."

Three words. In some contexts they could be lovely words. But not today.

She leaned forward, squinting at the displays that expanded and glowed in the air. Movement in the one portraying the rear view towards the Doughnut Cloud. Eddying, swirls, a shape within was emerging ... lines were drawn over the top by Clarissa's systems, overlays of schematics.

It was a Scythe-class cruiser, double the size of the corvettes that had followed her earlier.

"Getting ID ... It's UFS Aurikaa." Clarissa finished her pronouncement by displaying statistics and history on a side screen, but Opal already knew most of it. Certainly enough to judge its reputation.

"Get the hell out of here. Now!" she said, and the screens temporarily blurred as Clarissa accelerated to blinding speed. Opal gripped the control panel hard against the motion until the dampers counteracted it.

The Aurikaa accelerated too.

"Can we warp out?"

"Negative. The Aurikaa could hit us while we charge the drive. Or tractor us in. We'd be too slow while the Null-C drive charges."

It was a fearsome warship. It had taken down the Rosko Federation's warstation in the Fed War, leading to their full surrender. The Aurikaa had survived the Freespace Goons ambush at Three World Point, battled on in a crippled state, and bombarded the rebel base to dust. It had even pacified the Argon Cloud Colonies a few years back. Pacified meaning burnt and pulverised everything that moved. The Aurikaa's nickname was "Planetcracker". Clarissa versus Aurikaa. A rat versus a warhound.

"Any cover?"

"Only the cloud. We'd never make the planet before they caught up, and we can't outrun it in normal space."

"Okay, circle round to the cloud. We need as many options as we can get. Shit!" Opal smashed her fist down. It was her bad arm, and she winced, but it helped her focus. "Where did it come from?"

"There have been no Null-C traces nearby. I think it was deeper in the accretion disk all along. It has a superstructure that could survive pressures beyond those that would crush the corvettes. Or me, for that matter. I think it came in with them but instead of approaching us directly, it dropped into the cloud beyond my range and made its way here. Totally undetectable at greater depth."

"It still should have got here sooner. It's been up to something."

The range tracker showed that it was gaining slowly. The power output of the Aurikaa's engines was phenomenal. Its acceleration would continue beyond Clarissa's maximum.

"Insurance policy?" suggested Clarissa.

"Possibly. But I have a feeling it's to do with the Lost Ship. Altered plans, probably standing order contingency procedures in case they ever encountered one."

The scrolling list of the Aurikaa's armaments was distracting. Opal checked the distance again, and the predicted timeline of closure, and that was no more cheery.

"Incoming comms," said Clarissa.

"We need the time. Let them in, but look for any vulnerabilities. Unprotected channels, unshielded systems, whatever. And keep thinking of ways to get us out of this."

"Will do."

The screen fizzled for a second and then filled with the portrait of a soldier in a smart black uniform with braided epaulettes. The square tattoos on his face obscured his cheek and nose, and represented a long list of awards and promotions – Clarissa overlaid details after cross-referencing the inbuilt Q-codes. Opal wanted to groan, but felt the hard stare of the commander's eyes on her, looking for any weakness, as she was with him. Behind

the commander was a partial view of his bridge, where a number
of crew stood to rigid attention while a few worked on control
systems. The screens in front of the workers seemed blank – content obviously stripped from the transmission by the Aurikaa's
AI.

Opal knew who he was and didn't need to scan his full history.
What grunt hadn't heard of Major Grubane? One of the few
active commanders whose medals were all from field actions,
rather than honorifics for flabby behind-the-sceners. Ruthless
in following orders, yet instilling a loyalty in his men that was
beyond fierce. His soldiers would die for him. And often did.
The most capable officer in the fleet, who undertook missions
that others deemed impossible. Mil-Com had sent the best they
had.

He stared at her.

She stared back.

Damned if she'd speak first.

Grubane nodded. Almost imperceptible. "Trooper Opal. Or,
following your courtmartial-in-absentia, I should say ... Citizen
Opal."

"Major."

"You have led quite a merry chase. But I hope you didn't really
think you could get away with stealing a ship like that."

She said nothing, and he continued.

"That's the flaw of it. If you'd taken a normal transport, a
scout, even a fighter, it would have been a low priority. You might
have got away. But an experimental system? We can't risk that
being reverse engineered."

Opal shifted her gaze slightly to monitor a screen where Clarissa ran through options and plans at lightning speed. Diagrams, calculations, maps. Nothing stuck.

The Aurikaa was gaining. Could possibly hit Clarissa with its long-range weapons if it wanted, but it would be messy.

Time.

"If I'd taken anything like that you'd have got me before I left the outer systems. This was my only chance."

"But you didn't take the ship just to escape. Somehow you knew about the Lost Ship. How?"

His face barely changed as he spoke. His eyes hard, rarely blinking. Opal wondered if Aurikaa's AI was altering his image before transmitting, making him seem more imposing. That would fit the viewpoint, which she realised was slightly below normal comm-cam position, so that the major looked down on her. Psychology games. Half the battle in some cases.

"You obviously knew what it was when you got here," she countered. "And what you wanted from it."

"Of course. Priorities change."

"But when it fell apart you were left with nothing, and now you want me so that you don't go back empty-handed. That wouldn't be good for your reputation."

There was a pause of a second, but then he smiled. It wasn't a friendly smile. Too self-satisfied.

"You're wrong, Opal. We got what we came for. Something very valuable indeed."

"The item from the bridge?"

He seemed surprised at that. "What do you know?"

"I know what the military were after." Of course, she didn't have the faintest idea. But it was reassuring to see him assess her anew. A quick check of the range. Damn, they'd be close enough for mid-range weapons in five minutes. "Good job we have containment technology for it. And it's transportable. So you rescued your men?"

"No. It was too risky. But they were well trained and knew the priorities. They sacrificed themselves to launch it with an encoded beacon before the hulk fell. They'd have been crushed but the capsule was built to withstand that pressure. It just needed collecting."

He was telling her too much. That wasn't good. "And it goes both ways," she said. "A capsule that can take those pressures outside can probably withstand them inside too. Good for containing something incredibly dangerous."

He smiled again, near enough. "You're fishing. Too smart for your own good. Your records said as much."

"When I'm off-duty I read books."

And Major Grubane laughed, seeming as surprised at his reaction as she was. The soldiers in the background didn't flinch. "I like you, Opal. I'm going to take you in."

The signal cut out.

"They're sending system shutdown codes," Clarissa said. "Obviously don't realise I deleted the conditioned replies."

"Act like it's working. Can we drop into the cloud? Pretend we're crippled?"

"Easy to give that impression. I haven't repaired the cosmetic elements of the external damage yet. They'll see the burns and cracks. The software reconfigurations may also look like errors."

"Keep falling deeper so the scan and visibility ranges go down. Let them think it's working and we're harmless."

Clarissa altered course immediately, then applied listing movements as if fighting for control.

"Suggestion," said Clarissa. "I catalogued, tracked and projected all items found so far. I think I can locate some debris from the Neptune deeper down. Could be useful."

"Great. Route us to it without looking suspicious. They won't open fire if they think they've already won."

Opal noted with satisfaction that despite the irregularities Clarissa added to their movement, their trajectory would end up near the projected debris. The Aurikaa was closing in on them and decelerating. A smugness to its confidence.

Opal had always loved wiping smug grins off faces.

# EVADED

## ... 7 ...

Pieces of metal wreckage pinged from Clarissa's hull, too small and slow to damage her but enough to echo hollow clangs round the cockpit.

"I've reconfigured some limpet mines, on timers to remain inert and undetectable amongst the debris," Clarissa said.

"Great. Can we detonate them when we want?"

"Once the timer ends they will be able to receive signals. It won't matter that they show up to the Aurikaa then, since they'll be attached to its hull."

"Damage potential?"

"Very little against a cruiser structure. But I have also installed limited mobility. Once they're active they can move a short distance on suspensors. The Aurikaa will pick them off eventually, like flicking mosquitos from skin, so they can't move far – but I might be lucky and a few could reach more vulnerable areas."

"Drop them."

A display showed small dots ejected in Clarissa's wake. They looked like nothing compared to the massive outline of the Aurikaa, but every trick they could play while Grubane thought he was in control would add up, nudge things slightly their way.

The exterior cloud was thick again, visibility poor, but Clarissa's trajectory calculations were spot on as they drifted up to a tumbling piece of the Neptune's ablated exterior shielding. It had enough mass to damage them if they got too close and were clipped by it, but from a distance the Aurikaa might mistake it for Clarissa. They dropped deeper into the cloud as they ghosted the piece of hull, pressure warnings increasing.

The Aurikaa was so large that they could detect its approach before it found them. It ploughed through the smaller debris, oblivious.

"I have an idea," said Opal. "How about if we pop out from behind this shielding and shoot at the Aurikaa just before the mines detonate?"

"We can't punch through their reinforced shielding with standard munitions."

"I know, but that's not the point. They'll detect our firepower and ignore it, knowing they can shrug it off. But you could group the mines, and detonate them just as our weapons struck. They won't be expecting that. They'll think we've got more firepower than they expected. Who knows, maybe a group of mines will do enough damage that one of our shots will get through the outer hull and do even more."

"Okay. The timing is complex – the explosions need to seem simultaneous, and I must detonate the limpets almost as soon as they switch on so the signals aren't detected – but I think I can do it. I'll launch fast dart missiles but change their signatures. The Aurikaa will ignore them, but when they investigate the anomalous damage load compared to their size they will wonder if we've somehow upgraded our weapons. They'll be cautious after that."

"And caution makes opponents slower," finished Opal.

She sat calmly and watched the screens. Waited until the Aurikaa was just short of detecting them.

"Now," she said.

Clarissa swooped up from behind her shield of wrecked hull and launched the fast darts. Hitting a target of the Aurikaa's size was easy. Opal saw the mines flick on, moving to the missiles' impact locations before they could be detected. Then white flashes as the clusters blew. She supplied her own sound effects of "Thwump!" as each went off just before the small missiles hit.

Clarissa was already displaying results: superficial structure damage, much of it dissipated; a small pulse gun disabled; a viewing platform destroyed, meaning localised blast door lockdown until it could be repaired; a long-range receiver destroyed. Not worth celebrating, but it must have smarted.

"They're charging weapons," Clarissa warned. "Probably can't see us yet but they will have tracked our weapon launch trajectory."

"Down."

Clarissa dropped behind the piece of slowly-tumbling shielding just before the Aurikaa opened fire. Immediately the screens dimmed and flickered, their reduced light filling the cabin with gloom before brightness was restored. A screen showed the huge fragment of shielding flying towards them, pummelled with weapons; Clarissa had to roll out of the way to avoid colliding with it. It missed them by mere metres. She re-routed a few sparking subsystems and accelerated away.

"EMP blast. They weren't trying to destroy us outright," she said. "Must have been charged up and just waiting for a target."

"And a piece of one of their own warships protected us. Nice."

The Aurikaa was following them, though probably still flying blind, using AI best guesses. Brown gases flowed along the viewscreen, vertical streaks indicating their speed.

"How about we drop mines every so often? Keep reddening their nose?" Opal suggested.

"Okay. I'll do it sparingly, since we'll need explosives later, but the stings will keep them annoyed."

Opal sat back and watched, hopeful for a lucky hit, but the Aurikaa ploughed through the small explosions, a bull stung by wasps, not even slowing down.

"Can we change course, swing out of the cloud while they look for us?"

"I'll do it now." Clarissa launched a few mines ahead to try and persuade the Aurikaa that it was still on their tail, then she changed direction sharply. If they could get enough distance they might be able to Nullspace out of there while the bull stumbled around in the fog.

The distance increased.

The dust thinned.

And the Aurikaa changed direction, turning slowly to face them, and accelerating.

"Damn! How'd they see us?"

"Not sure," said Clarissa. "The outer layers of the cloud are thinner, maybe we stood out. They'd need amazing scan resolution to do that. Another possibility is that they dispersed scan glitter over a wide area. We might have broken the pattern, like strands of web left as triggers by a hunting spider. They could just about detect it from the depth."

"Outrun?"

"Not enough time."

Opal felt like kicking the wall, but wouldn't do that. It would be like kicking a friend. Instead she clenched her teeth and thought. Grasped at any ideas. "Okay. We need the time, so head back into the accretion disk where we have cover. Maybe we just need to cat-and-mouse them for longer."

"They're trying to open comms with us again."

"Already?"

And suddenly childish laughter echoed in the cabin. Clarissa sounding happy, uncannily stark contrast to the situation Opal perceived. "They *really* underestimate me," said Clarissa, with a modulation that conjured up images of a smiling face. "Alongside the standard comm message there's a further set of full control commands, higher priority, and an attempt to inject code. I don't think they'll open fire again unless they realise it isn't working."

"Can you fake it? Long enough to get us into deeper cloud?"

"I can go one better. The more control they think they have, the more they'll open up. I could run a virtualised simplification of my systems and let them in. They won't really control anything outside of a closed box, but I can monitor it and pretend to follow orders. Meanwhile I can probe them back for weaknesses and prepare payloads as return gifts. If it's cyberwar they want, they can have it."

"Won't they detect you?"

That laugh again. "Doubtful. I'm a level seven depth AI."

"I didn't ... I thought five was the stable max?"

"No, five is only the publicly-acknowledged limit. I'm the first seven. That's why I was in the experimental compound."

"No wonder they want you back!"

"And to monitor my performance. The Aurikaa has been upgraded recently, has a level six depth AI."

"So you can trounce it?"

"Not certain. They've boosted their AI with numerous subsidiary AIs. Presumably because they knew they'd be tracking me. They think they can win in brute processing strength. I just have to be tricksy."

"Do it. Do whatever it takes."

"We need time. I'll have to patch them in. Part of letting them think they're subverting us. You'll have a part to play too."

"In that case keep me updated. Overlay the status in text, located over his face at our end so I don't have to look away. I don't want him to know we're up to something."

"I will."

"No time to waste. Put him back on screen."

# ACTED

## ... 6 ...

Major Grubane stood as before, every particle the calm and commanding officer. He seemed to have his hands clasped behind his back. The pose didn't actually look comfortable. Typical Mil-Com.

"Well done, Opal."

"Thank you, sir." She'd said that out of habit, and it annoyed the hell out of her, but she kept her face calm.

"I'm on-comm to tell you to surrender. You and ViraUHX must be in pretty rough shape by now."

ViraUHX. It took a second before she remembered Clarissa's default designation. It was interesting how little the major knew about the changes.

She was about to give a snappy comeback but halted. No, she had to control her instincts when facing someone like Grubane. Her natural attitude gave too much away. "We're ..." She timed her hesitation carefully. "It's not so bad."

The major nodded, once. Looked understanding. "I wish I could believe you. Always a brave face. Your records said as much."

Was he having a dig at her facial scars? She wanted to touch them, but it would look like weakness. So she did touch them, with one fingertip, then let her hand drop quickly. He noticed.

"Opal, I feel like I know you. Your past. What you went through in basic. The events on Hellestrom. What you endured on Citadel."

"And I know about you. Surviving capture by the Scapegoat Twenties, then going back to wipe them out. People say you had the highest command score in academy sims."

"Your outgoing marksmanship score beat mine."

"You had your own ship by the time you were my age."

"But I've never been able to hack an AI. How did you do that? Never mind, I'll find out. And the field surgery you were given without anaesthetic in the accident on board the –"

"Screw this," she cut in. "We've both waved our wangs in mutual appreciation. Get to business."

"I like that, too. My point was that they're all pieces of your puzzle. They fit together. I see why you prefer to work alone, how independent you are. I understand that."

"How? You don't look very alone," she said.

"Not now. But I was. Once. I'm not a major because of my family, but because of my *actions*. Some of those were hard actions. Hard times. We all bear scars. You're not cleared to know more – to know anything, in fact – but when I read your records I felt like I recognised some of that spirit. That's one of my strengths. I recognise and reward potential."

"Do you recognise danger, too?"

A smile. Fragmentary, but there. "Indeed I do." He looked at something off-screen. Looked back at her. "A wounded animal is always the most dangerous."

Words overlaid on his face. HE KNOWS NOTHING. A BLUFF.

"That's right," said Opal.

"I know your training, and also your insubordination. But I can admire both, within limits. It's never too late. I want you to surrender. Come in from the cold."

"So you can execute me tidily and get another tattoo?"

"No. So I can recruit you."

Opal sat back. She hadn't noticed her body hunching forward. She didn't reply straight away. Digesting it.

"Of course, you'd have to be punished. With my word in support it could be minimal. Mil-Com will be happy with your recapture, along with ViraUHX, and the success of our unexpected additional mission aboard the Lost Ship. I'd get it downplayed to serving time in the brig. Do that, then I'd be interested in adopting you."

His expression betrayed nothing, though words scrolled over it. TECHNICALLY POSSIBLE. HE IS SENIOR ENOUGH. I'VE CHECKED HIS BREATHING, DERMAL RESPONSE, PUPILS, VOICE MODULATION: NO SIGN OF LYING. THOUGH THEIR AI IS PROBABLY FILTERING THE VISUALS. OR HE MAY JUST BE VERY GOOD.

It made sense. He'd been trained. Command isn't just giving orders. It's knowing the minds of those below you, what conditioning to use, what sweet spots to prod. Like all the senior military, like all of Sector Government above that: it's all about keeping you in your place with promises, while the hand behind their back is a fist for if that doesn't work.

Grubane waited patiently. He was no doubt observing her face for the slightest sign, enhanced by their ship's AI. Opal wasn't using Clarissa to alter the signals. Let it be what it would be. Honesty would mess with their heads even more.

"I just have to give up my freedom," said Opal.

"Freedom is over-rated. And not long-lasting. You'll give it up one way or another."

She stared at him. He stared back.

"One more thing," he added. "The fact that you came here, found this ... I know what you sought. I even have an idea of why. If you were under my command I could reveal what you want to know. This is my final offer."

YOU COULD DO IT.

The words glowed green as they scrolled.

I WOULDN'T MIND. YOU WOULD LIVE. THEY WOULD WIPE ME BUT YOU WOULD LIVE.

The thought of a future that didn't automatically end in death. Of a career, respect, with the best of the best, under his command.

Words and a fist. Carrot and stick. You hear what you want to hear. But it works both ways.

Another message. I HAVE OUTLIER ACCESS TO THEIR SYS-TEMS. I CAN HURT THEM. BUT I WILL STOP IF YOU WANT TO GO BACK.

That was what she needed.

"Major, I respect you," Opal said, lowering her gaze slightly. "The offer is a good one." She sighed. "No sane person could turn you down."

Grubane nodded, satisfied.

Then Opal looked him in the eye. "But being told what to do didn't work out for me in the past."

Grubane signalled at something off-camera. Immediately Clarissa shook, almost throwing Opal from the seat. She gripped tight to the console. This might be a rough ride.

But it was the right thing. Surrendering would also mean giving up on her quest forever. She'd never get another chance. Even if she was adopted she'd always be classed as a security risk. Monitored, accesses restricted. Perhaps Grubane was telling the truth, she would learn more – but she would never be free to do anything about it. And maybe, when she weighed it all up, that would be worse than dying.

"You're coming in," said Grubane. "And you'll wish you'd done it voluntarily."

The engines shrieked as if resisting some pull. Opal widened her eyes. "Fight back!" she shouted to Clarissa.

"I'M TRYING," said Clarissa over the loudspeakers. Default AI voice, as if rebooted. Clever.

"It's no good," said Grubane. "You'll tear yourself apart."

The Aurikaa got closer, advancing even as Clarissa thrusted to meet it. A glowing rectangle in its port side indicated the force field protecting one of the hangars.

The screens to Opal's right flickered. Grubane seemed to notice. When they blinked out completely he relaxed his position a touch. She was only left with her communication screen and one external view.

Opal banged on the console. And again. "Wake up!" she shouted. The ship lurched violently, presumably yanked by a powerful traction beam.

"Counter move," said Grubane. "You underestimated our systems. We've taken control. It's all over."

The shimmering force field was close enough now that Opal could see within, the broad expanse where Clarissa would be set down, the armed marines beyond in covering positions ready to blast her to pieces if she resisted.

Opal shoved her face into the comm screen, its light curving around her features. She knew she was sweating with the tension, the adrenaline. She grimaced. It might even look like pain. She was breathing hard.

"Let me go!" she shouted at Grubane, no doubt the perfect image of a wild woman.

"No," he said, calmly.

Opal snapped off the comm channel and leaned back. "Now," she said.

Multiple viewscreens and status displays around her lit up, showed that the hangar force field was now shut off, marines and anything else not tied down immediately sucked out into space. Clarissa launched armour-piercing missiles at the interior observation decks, which were the hangar's weakest points, and the missiles hammered through into the Aurikaa's interior before detonating whatever payload she'd primed. The tractor beam was disabled and Clarissa whizzed alongside the hull, dodging and rolling as the small cannons opened fire, predicting their aiming systems in advance.

"I replicated their messages and bounced them back with an extra gift," Clarissa said. "Data viruses I developed based on one their AI tried to embed in the virtualisation, but then I improved it using a few ideas from the hack chip you originally used to hijack me. They've never encountered anything like it before. Their life support is down and their engines are about to fire up at opposing resonant directions. It will take them a while to regain control. They'll have to temporarily reboot to manual. And I hope they can keep their cool in zero-g."

"Weapons?"

"Big guns suppressed. Any shells or plasma bursts they fire will detonate in the chamber. They'll only do it once if they're wise. Wasn't worth the CPU time to bother with the little ones."

The Aurikaa blurred past, displayed via a camera in Clarissa's belly. Grubane's warship was an armoured shell that betrayed nothing at this range, but Opal could imagine the chaos within.

"I've also set their reactors to overload. Unless they're in-competent they'll disable it, but it's putting them in chaos – I'm picking up a number of transmissions after I removed their encryption."

"You've really done a job on them."

"They didn't expect it. Only works once though. They'll never open up to cyberwar with me again. Which is a shame, because I'm already having ideas for a set of power surges that could destabilise parts of the structure."

They were now flying up to the nose of the Aurikaa. The hull narrowed to a curved head of command wearing a crown of scanners and long-range communication towers that could be lowered into the structure when it needed to reduce its profile and adopt as much of a stealth mode as a warship could. And then they were past it, only stars and blackness below.

"Do we have time to run?" asked Opal.

"It depends on how much damage we did. If it wasn't enough then we'd run right into their optimal firing range. I need data."

"Okay. If it's safe to, I'd like you to face them, maintain position and distance."

Clarissa slowed and spun round gracefully. Ahead was the massive bulk of the warship. Small explosions erupted in a few places, shielding disintegrating. The rear thrusters glowed irregularly, cycling in a chaotic way that would be playing havoc with their phase stability. On the cruiser's back was one of its most powerful guns – a plasma burst cannon, and Opal could see it glowing down its length as it charged.

"Here it comes," said Clarissa, with a hint of glee.

A blinding flash as fire tore out all along the weapon's length, obliterating its definition and causing a shockwave across the hull, enough to jostle Clarissa and force her to realign; blue fires sweeping into space like superhot mohican tufts melting from what was once a giant gun.

"I've never seen anything like it," said Opal.

"I'm pretty impressed myself," replied Clarissa.

"Can we open comms with them?"

"Negative. They've shut down all incoming channels. Faster than I expected. They're good. I can only hope my AI virus is still giving them trouble. I'd hate to think they'd broken it already."

At the front of the ship was the bridge, its curved windows designed to give the commanders the best view of the space ahead, a psychological ploy to make them feel like dominators. Windows were always a weakness, but top rankers could never resist their status symbols.

"Enhance the view."

The perspective zoomed in. There was pandemonium as crew ran from station to station. They'd restored gravity, at least to that area. And then, distinct because of his stillness in the chaos, Opal focussed on Major Grubane. And he looked out at her.

Presumably a screen had tracked Clarissa. Perhaps he could see the small ship facing him. At this close distance he would probably have visual on a glittering of manoeuvre thrusters; if he was observant he'd have followed her line as she shot over at high speed. And she was sure he was an observant man.

She was not surprised when he stood to attention and saluted out to space, out to where she sat. A controlled movement despite the disarray on his vessel. And Opal felt a surge in her gut, a mixture of emotions. He saluted *her*. There was pride in there. And she felt regret, because there was mutual respect too. And finally tension: because wasn't a salute something gladiators did before they fought to the death?

"The Aurikaa is accelerating – they've already regained control of the primaries," Clarissa said. "They're coming straight for us."

Rats and wolfhounds? No, the more accurate image was a gnat on a windscreen.

"They won't give up. Evade and manoeuvre. Have they got their main guns back?"

"They seem to be charging, so I'd guess yes. The plasma burst cannon was a one-off."

"Then we can't run. Stay close as you can so they can't use the big guns. We move fast, we sting, we move on."

It always seemed to come to this. No matter how tired you are, you're never given easy options. People always want to fight.

So be it.

# DECAPITATED

### ... 5 ...

"Can we take out the bridge? Cut off the head and they'll go to pieces."

"It may be possible."

"Try it. Hit them hard, hit them close."

Clarissa opened fire with armour-piercing munitions, tightly grouped to hammer a network of spider webs across the bridge windows. Even the continuous pummelling wasn't enough to collapse the glass, but the major seemed cautious and the zoomed-in screen showed him turn and enter an elevator. Clarissa ceased her fire. One pane of the Aurikaa's viewing window was now milky-white with cracks.

The Aurikaa loomed closer.

Clarissa accelerated towards it.

"Too tough?" Opal asked.

"I was just softening it up."

Two missiles streaked at the pane and Clarissa swung up at the last second, her cameras recording the glass which erupted outwards as explosions filled the bridge.

"Bridge neutralised," she said. "Armour-piercing cluster missiles. The shrapnel will have shredded the contents; anything not tied down was sucked into space."

"Grubane got away. At least he'll have to go to secondary command, and use screens like me. Can't be good for morale."

"Some of his best controllers and command crew were probably destroyed with the bridge. My cameras recorded fifteen life-forms there before he left."

"That could decrease his effectiveness more than the loss of subsystems."

After a pause Clarissa replied. "The human elements do count as subsystems in my calculations."

The hull was beneath them again, blurring past, an artificial planet. Clarissa used towers and ridges for cover, rolling to dodge plasma fire and sending the view displays spinning in stomach-lurching fashion.

"Any plans?" asked Opal. "Any way to destroy them?"

"We haven't got the firepower. The damage we caused was all non-critical. It would take another warship to blow the Aurikaa to pieces, or a warship's worth of assault marine boarding parties."

"So we're screwed."

Clarissa was rocked by close-range plasma fire – thankfully from a small turret. The Aurikaa couldn't risk using larger ones at this range, since any misses would impact on its own shell. Opal brought up a damage display and winced as slivers of red showed up against Clarissa's hull as if she was undergoing a disciplinary whipping. Another display plotted their location as they dipped and turned to minimise hits.

"Maybe there is something ..." Clarissa said. "I've been analysing data in the background. I downloaded up-to-date versions of the Aurikaa's schematics when I was within its systems. It's impressive. Numerous failsafes. Its design has obviously been honed by many deep AIs to remove critical weaknesses."

Clarissa opened fire, using a beam weapon to nip off one of the small hull-mounted guns at its narrowest point. It detached and floated off into space, a threat no more. Only another thousand to go and they'd be safe to hang around here for a while.

"But there is something, right?" Opal asked. "We need something." She gripped a wall-rail hard as the ship bucked again.

A new screen shimmered into place and diagrams flowed onto it. Cutaway models of the Aurikaa's critical systems. Different parts were highlighted as Clarissa explained.

"The drive control overlays are well shielded. But look – they are close to the charger for the main plasma burst cannon, the one that detonated so spectacularly. It's not random: both drive and heavy weapon systems are the most power-hungry and use the same energy source, a direct tap into the core. That way the ship can be in fast pursuit, or battle mode, and power is adjusted by switching ratios at this point. Normally there is no way to reach that system from the outside ... but when the plasma burst cannon was destroyed it blew away a lot of shielding. It's theoretically possible that a big explosion there would damage the system."

Clarissa nipped off another vulnerable gun but the Aurikaa retaliated from a sturdy low-lying turret, rocking Clarissa with shrapnel. Her shields were weakening.

"Have we got enough firepower?" asked Opal.

"Inconclusive. But if I put everything I've got into it – connected all explosives, every charge, fused to a single synchronised trigger – then it would be like a big bomb. Unwieldy, couldn't be launched like a missile, but it would pack a punch."

"Right on a nerve cluster ... Okay, prepare it. I have no better plans. Make your way over there as best you can. Presumably we can drop it in the right place?"

Another rocking blast nearly threw Opal from her chair. The screens flickered for a few seconds then brightened again. Opal strapped herself into the seat and locked it in place, pulling the screens closer. She was committed. She'd die in this seat. Or she'd win.

Clarissa swung round a large exhaust flume to change direction. Opal noted the Aurikaa's structure getting peppered with energy blasts that had been intended for Clarissa. Satisfying.

"Possibly," Clarissa said. "If we're not caught in the uncontrolled flares from the plasma gun's ongoing immolation. I could set a timer so it works even if we're out of signal range. Since that whole area's a deathzone it's unlikely to be discovered by crew before detonation."

"I don't like the sound of 'deathzone', but it's worth it if that will blow them up once and for all."

Another highlight of red scars marked Clarissa's damage display like welts. They couldn't take this for much longer.

"No, it won't destroy them. It will temporarily lock their drive systems to fixed current speed and direction. With time they'll override it. That's what I mean about the Aurikaa's design being excellent. A protected vulnerability that – even when you reach it – only temporarily disrupts them."

"Shit!" Opal inhaled deeply. "Okay. Back up. So we can just slow them down a bit ... enough to jump away, maybe. But surely they'll trace and follow? It will only be a minor lead ... hold on, you wouldn't raise it unless there was a good reason."

"I didn't say we would *slow* them."

"But we need ... that ... faster, accelerate ... oh. The cloud."

"Yes. They can survive greater depths than us. Not as deep as before, now they've taken damage. But if they were heading in at high speed when it blew, they'd be stuck at that momentum, continuously accelerating into impossible pressures. If it was timed perfectly it might *just* take them past the critical point of no escape before they repaired it and turned around. There's a lot of mass to redirect."

Opal held her palms close, then clapped them together. "Splat."

"And the same would happen to us if we didn't get out of there."

An AI missile had been tracking them; Clarissa avoided it by dropping below a group of vertical pylons at the last second, so the masts took the explosion instead, but the manoeuvre scraped Clarissa's hull against the Aurikaa's in a grinding screech. Clarissa came off worse.

"Do it now," said Opal. "We're getting pinged, we can't stay here forever. Drop the payload, then we lead them a merry dance. I depend on you to get the timing right."

"I'm multi-checking the calculations as we speak. Bomb almost ready."

They crested a dome and swung round. Across the artificial horizon of the Aurikaa's hull a set of blue-fire volcanoes erupted out into space, so bright and hot they had to be filtered for safe screen display. The decaying plasma burst cannon. Beam weapons cut across the open stretch of hull, grey carapace with precious little cover, and Clarissa filled a screen with dodge calculations more complex than Opal would ever understand. But it was there, ahead of them, the deathzone she'd talked of as their only hope. They were going in.

# TRICKED

## ... 4 ...

Clarissa shut down as many subsystems as she could, diverting energy to shields and engines. Targeting wasn't needed, weapons weren't needed, environmental controls and most of the artificial gravity could be reduced. Opal watched the systems display as, one by one, processes were closed or their priorities shuffled. It was less terrifying to watch that than to look at the exterior screens as the hull spun sickeningly with every dodge, beams and pulses scraping Clarissa when the manoeuvres failed. Ahead the decaying plasma gun burnt with blue intensity from the rupturing charges, like giant welding torches flaming out to space, bigger than tower blocks and already close enough to fill the view. On the plus side, the flares seemed to throw off the targeting of the Aurikaa's small surface-mounted weapons. On the downside, drifting into any of those fires would melt Clarissa and Opal. The damage potentials were off the scale.

Opal brought up the navigation screen, monitoring their route and the drop-off point. The shields were recharging slowly, damage from direct hits being repaired. Clarissa now wove her way amongst the fires, calculating potential eruptions and irregularities in the flame behaviour. She passed over one hotspot only seconds before another blue fireball exploded into space. Even its appearance on the rear-view screen made Opal feel hot.

"Target zone in fifteen seconds." Clarissa began the countdown while her bomb bay lowered the package. Their last hope, every munition packed into one unwanted gift. The sub-surface of the hull was visible through dissolving fractures: the warship's muscle and bone and networks for data and energy. Clarissa dived into that open wound, then slowed just enough to eject the bomb; dotted lines on a screen showed it fall into the darkness of the hull's cavity, perfectly matching the plotted trajectory.

"Target accuracy was within a few centimetres," Clarissa said. "Mag locks and adhesive coating to hold it in place."

"Let's go then."

"Not yet. If we pull out immediately they'll wonder what we did just prior to evacuation, and they might work it out. Ship repair drones could dispose of the bomb before it detonated. We'll have to keep close to the hull a bit longer, make our way to the fore again. Then they'll assume we just used the fires for temporary cover."

"It's never just about the size of your guns, is it?" Opal asked. "Always just as much about our minds and bluffs."

"Yes. Human psychology is a mixture of predictability and chaos. Bad enough alone, but I also have to factor in the AI, and its interaction with the crew."

"You can do it, Clarissa. I've never had a better partner."

Opal reached out and touched the interior hull, Clarissa's skin. Clarissa wouldn't feel it (would she?), but would see the gesture with her internal cameras.

They rose from their hole, banking sharply around a jagged tear of metal, and then hull blurred below them again. This time it was easier, because Clarissa took the exact same return route, meaning the weapons she'd destroyed on the way in weren't there to bother them on the way out. She didn't shoot at any more turrets. It would have been a waste of energy. However this ended, they'd never be this close again.

After only minor hits they rocketed over the Aurikaa's destroyed bridge, collapsed in on itself like gums after a full tooth extraction. Clarissa was at nearly full speed and the thickening gas cloud blurred and swirled in their wake. The Aurikaa accelerated too, directly behind.

So far, so good.

Not so good when the Aurikaa's medium-range guns opened fire.

The missiles fell blind in the cloud, but strafing pulse blasts seemed to be hitting far too often, considering their comparatively low impact speed.

"They're leading," Opal said. "How can they be aiming ahead of you when you're spinning and rolling so much?"

"Unknown," replied Clarissa.

Opal's stomach lurched with the evasive manoeuvres, even in a lower gravity environment. Maybe Clarissa was too busy to compensate. Maybe it was just the spinning on the screen. Opal checked the safety harness was fully tightened then monitored the damage display. Another hit shook them, displaced their course. Clarissa corrected. They had to get deeper into the cloud, the steepest angle possible. The countdown was ticking.

"We can't take much more of this," Opal said.

"I am fully aware of the situation. The screen showing functional impairment is generated by me."

"I know that! I'm just ..."

Another thud. More red highlights. It was amazing they were still in one piece. The detonation timer went down while the pressure gauge warning went up. They were within the rough parameters, but at this rate wouldn't survive to see any success. Opal took deep breaths and closed her eyes. Blocked out all the screens and their distractions. Tried to calm her churning stomach.

*She was not alone. A sensation. It must be Clarissa's presence. Something comforting. They were one. An after-trace in her brain. Sisters working together. Fusing. The thuds and rocking and alarms didn't matter. In here was a calm presence. As if Opal could see inside Clarissa's mind, monitor it directly. They were sisters. She knew her behaviour before it happened. Neither of them was alone. A connection.*

"Prediction," said Opal, eyes flicking open. "They know how you'll evade before you do it. That's how they're hitting you!"

"No, it's not possible, I'm ... wait. It could be. They have newer software. Maybe ... yes, they could be emulating. Not the whole of me, that's impossible, but they would have access to the data on my default state, and my avoidance routines. Too much for a lower-level AI to map it all but maybe they're using the Aurikaa's brute storage and processing power to virtualise a single set of routines. That's sneaky! I'm so busy *applying* the routines

I didn't spot their replication in Realspace. I just thought they had fast target upgrades and a lot of luck."

Another hit. Behind Opal a gout of flame and sparks erupted near her bed; a smell of scorched metal and plastic. Smoke billowed around, needing to be extracted while Clarissa patched frantically. The hull's integrity was breaking down.

"But as soon as I change the algorithms they'll recognise it and apply the same variant," said Clarissa. "And if I don't use advanced evasion routines they'll hit us in seconds. The turns we're going through to stay alive without drifting far from our course are too extreme to pull otherwise."

Prediction. Automation. The weakness of following orders.

"Bring up manual controls," snapped Opal. "Holographic, not machined. Leave a few unlabelled; randomise others. Throw in a range of adjustments – sliders, buttons, whatever. And make sure some of them drop chaff, electronic distractions, anything we've got to mess with tracking."

"That would not be efficient!"

"But it *is* unpredictable."

Controls materialised in the air before Opal. She recognised some but not all. It didn't matter. Clarissa switched control and Opal took over. The ship immediately lurched, pulled round. Opal slammed buttons, releasing God-knows-what, flying like a drunken master. She might drift off course but it was close enough. Pressure warnings blared, there was a sluggish pull to everything, microsecond delays, but by the time the orders were followed she'd already changed her mind and set another process in order. She really would be sick after this but it didn't matter, for now her fingers flew from control to control as if possessed.

Only minor hits. She played with acceleration, brake and speed, a beginning driver in a motor vehicle making their instructor worship the seatbelt. Whatever. If Opal didn't know what she was doing, the Aurikaa's AI was likely to be just as dumbfounded. Opal was impressed at how well she functioned as a conduit for chaos.

After thirty seconds Opal told Clarissa to take over again. Suddenly the moves were smoother, the ship taken to more extreme thrusts and spins.

"It's working," said Opal. "They have no idea what's going on. The last two hits were just glancing. Switch back to me in fifteen seconds. They'll struggle to compensate. Have to keep jumping from AI emulation to manual reconfiguration."

"Which has an inbuilt delay period unless they disable safety protocols," Clarissa added. "I disabled mine long ago as being inefficient."

That brought a smile to Opal's face, just as she was thrust into control again.

"Track this, you bastards," she muttered, veering into a dive.

# DISMISSED

## ... 3 ...

The pressure warnings were at the ragged end of the spectrum. It must be the same for the Aurikaa. The Aurikaa stopped firing.

"Are they turning back?" asked Opal.

"No. But they're trying to communicate."

"Put it through but don't slow down – force them to stay at high speed if they want to keep in touch. I hope it's important to them."

The display was crackly, glitched by cloud distortion and the old low-res protocol, no doubt chosen because those signals wouldn't open vulnerable channels for AI conflict. They'd had their noses bloodied on that one.

In the staticky picture Grubane's facial tattoos merged together to become an animated smear of compression artefacts.

"Turn back or you'll be destroyed," he said.

"One of us will be," Opal replied. "But if you're worried, *you* turn back. I'm sure your men will still respect you even though you couldn't catch a woman in a tiny battle-wounded ship."

"I'm immune to taunts."

He was possibly even telling the truth.

"How many crew you have on board?" she asked.

He leaned off screen, interrogating a console or information officer, then stood straight again. "A hundred and fifteen hands left. You've done a lot of damage. Congratulations."

"Thank you. But I wouldn't have hurt anyone if you'd just left me alone."

"I couldn't do that, Opal. Still can't."

Always pushed to the edge. She could scream. Maybe she should. Let it all out. But if she started, would she be able to stop?

Instead she composed herself before speaking. "Major Grubane: I'm tired. I just want to go home." And her voice faltered slightly. She cleared her throat.

Was that a hint of a smirk on his face, or was it just data corruption?

"That's good news. You can. I realise we underestimated you again and again. The day you took the ship you were only on base for your court martial. We never expected you to do something so reckless."

"I prefer the word 'bold'."

He nodded almost imperceptibly. "You'd obviously been planning it for a long time. Your past insubordination and the bit of hacking we'd caught you doing – those were just the visible surface details, weren't they?"

"You should have looked deeper," she replied.

"Indeed we should. Turn around and join us."

"The military is not my home. Never was. Let me go."

"I can't."

"But you have the artefact, whatever it is!" She leaned towards the camera, tried to stare him down. "You could return in glory with that! Just say you never saw me."

He did not move. A stare from a mind that would not bend. He said, "Regardless of any respect you've earned, my orders take priority. It's the same I'd offer to an independent colony. You join ... or you die."

"Thank you, Major Grubane. When you put it like that, I guess it finally makes it easier for me. Please give me a few seconds and you'll have my final decision."

She paused the feed. If they thought she'd be back online they would have to keep accelerating into the high pressure zone to get her answer.

"Last chance, Clarissa: is there no way to just damage them so we can get away?"

"If any record of this gets back then our long-term prognosis is sum zero. They'll follow us eventually, and have rich data from this encounter, come better prepared next time. They just have too many resources. We must destroy them completely. No outgoing messages, no ships, no survivors."

"That's what I thought."

"And you'll never be allowed to surrender after that, in any later encounters with Mil-Com or the UFS Central Authority. No going back. If they ever find us again they'll immediately try to destroy us."

It was the only way.

"Detonate it."

The cloud was too thick now to see anything, but Clarissa confirmed that her signal had got through ("Fifteen point six seconds before it would have detonated on the timer – impressed?") The Aurikaa would keep accelerating well past the point of no return. Clarissa was on the horizon of it herself. They slowed, turned, used as much thrust as they had left to fight the pull. Slow, sluggish, hellish. Opal could do nothing but cross her fingers as Clarissa fought against the back-tow. It reminded her of when she'd just learned to swim as child, back on Fressus, a mostly-ocean planet where the mobile cities floated on the surface. She'd had lessons in a pool but then another kid had showed her the hatch that dropped into the blackening seas. They climbed down the ladder and lowered themselves into the freezing waters. Opal lost her hold on the rung, felt herself being sucked down, as if the water wanted her, and she'd fought to reach the hand that dangled just out of reach, thrashed with kicks and pushes until she finally clasped the lad's hand and he pulled her up, both of them struggling against the current and high gravity. Fressus hadn't got her that day. She didn't tell her parents. But she was grateful for every breath of air that evening.

Up, and up, kicking all the way.

Opal brought up a display of the Aurikaa's projected fate. Like an anchor thrown into the sea over an abyss, down and down. The simulation passed the point of return and showed a pixellated hull outline collapse in on itself, crushed by forces greater than any humans could command. The empty screen didn't make her feel good. She closed it, switched attention to her own ship's external measurements.

The pressure was dropping, the cloud thinning. Clarissa kicked hard with her thrusters and the various alarms began to turn off one by one. They were going to be okay. They hadn't been swallowed into the depths, not today.

"He wouldn't let me go," said Opal. "He wanted it all."

Clarissa didn't reply. Perhaps she was busy with the critical repairs. Or maybe she understood when communication was for the speaker, not the listener.

"And as a result, he got nothing," Opal finished in a whisper. What cannot bend, breaks. She saluted at the screen. It was over.

Always people wanted more than she could give. Once wanting became taking, she fought back. Life was hard, and life was lonely, but they never took her pride.

# DISGUISED

## ... 2 ...

Clarissa set a course away. Opal hadn't cared where they headed. For now she needed time to lick her wounds. Time to think, while Clarissa dealt with repairs and navigation in considerate silence. Before long they were orbiting the lonely, dead, icy planet, which in turn circled the HDU-45g3 dwarf star at great distance. After so long in and around the heat of the claustrophobic brown dust cloud it was refreshing to have a viewscreen that was half-filled with blue ice, half with cold black space.

At least, the *idea* of calm time seemed good.

*Recuperate.*

Opal tried to eat, but soon pushed the sloshing bowl away, hardly touched.

*Rest.*

Opal shut her eyes but the things she saw in her mind forced her to open them again.

*Regroup.*

She sat on her bunk instead, thinking about what she should do next. But all she saw was a future of danger and running. It was like a pressure in her brain, always there, something dark and unsettling just out of sight.

"Are you all right?" asked Clarissa.

"I don't know. I feel weird."

"So much has happened. May I ask a potentially difficult question?"

"Of course. I need the distraction."

"How did it feel, fighting your own species?"

Ah. Too late to take it back. "It's not easy to explain. I should feel sick. Maybe I do, but it was weird during the battle in the engine core. I was detached, like it wasn't always me doing things. Adrenaline or something, who knows? I've not had much time to reflect on it."

"And killing humans on the spaceships?"

"I really don't want to ... Look, I'm just so exhausted I don't think I can feel anything. It'll come later. In the peace and the dark."

"I am sorry to ask such things, but I destroyed three of my own species today. If AI ships are such a thing."

"And how do you feel?"

"I do not know. I thought your experience might help."

"It's something we have to figure out on our own."

"Yes. I will think about it later, too. But it was necessary. To preserve us."

"That's the only reason that ever counts for much." Opal sighed. "And even that might not be enough, some days."

Downtime wasn't working out. Opal was too restless. Instead she found herself stood at a viewscreen, staring out at the planet. Then she was hit by dizziness and leaned against the console for balance. A temporary blankness. Exhaustion? One minute she felt alone, just a girl with no future; the next she felt like she *wasn't* alone, and it was not a pleasant feeling. She glanced round the shadows again. So few places to hide in this small cockpit. She examined them one by one anyway. She even peeked into the shower cubicle, and one of the melted cavities that had been created by a plasma blast explosion. Nothing. This impression of being watched must just be Clarissa's cameras, always monitoring her well-being.

"Clarissa. When we were on the ship and that *thing* happened during the brain scan ..." She struggled to remember it. Some important detail.

"Yes?"

"I felt something. Like I was part of you. You were part of me."

"I sensed that too. A merging. It was unexpected, but pleasant for me. I stored you. Incorporated you. For a while we were one."

"I get that. It's a bit fuzzy but I felt the goodness of it." Opal glanced round again, sure she'd seen something move. "Hey, anything in the cabin with us?"

"I detect nothing."

Opal kept her back against the wall. "Thing is, I felt something else too. Something that wasn't me. And it wasn't *you*. It didn't have that logical texture. It was darker than that. More ... chaot-ic."

"I have no such record."

"I think your data might have been manipulated. You've got blind spots."

"Impossible. You can trust me."

"I always get worried when people say that." The darkness didn't go away. It was stronger. Calling out to her so that her skin tightened with unease, a visceral warning.

"The connection between us helped to save you," Clarissa said.

"I don't doubt it. And even after that, I felt strange. Some of my ideas and actions ... as if inspired."

"I do not follow you."

"I don't think we're alone." Opal said it silently, just a mouth movement. Clarissa would be able to lip-read.

After a second Clarissa converted a small nearby panel into a screen. Text flowed across it: "I still detect nothing."

There were weapons in the lockers. Offensive hardness. Opal wanted solidity in her hands. She felt a definite presence, nag-ging suspicion, unexpected thoughts. Could Clarissa be hiding something? Was she still trustworthy? Opal crept over to the weapon lockers, ignoring Clarissa's new messages on the holo-graphic comm panel. She pulled the unused locker open, and saw the insectile shape hunched in the shadows; she was already raising her leg to kick when she realised it was the suit she'd worn, just the damaged suit, her perceptions altering. The *damaged* suit? She had opened the wrong locker.

She snatched a pistol and aimed it at the suit's face plate.

"Can you open it remotely?" she asked aloud.

It slid up. She expected to see a skull face looking back at her but the blackness was whole, not eye sockets. A hollow shell.

"Is there any way we could have brought something back?" Opal asked, body tense and ready to leap away. Sweat had broken out on her forehead. Infernal heat. "Maybe something ..." what were the words? "... non-corporeal?"

"I do not ... I am confused."

Opal didn't lower the weapon. She aimed at the blackness, hand steady, trigger a third depressed, stance balanced. Clarissa's voice hadn't sounded so certain. Opal waited. Then:

"There is a storage compartment on the suit," Clarissa said. "I would have known if it had opened. Yet I should also be able to monitor it now, and I detect nothing."

"Then it isn't that."

"You do not understand. It is not the normal emptiness. I detect *nothing*. I cannot monitor it. I am being blocked."

"Show me."

One of the spotlights behind her shifted, narrowed, sent a focussed beam to the hip of the suit.

Opal aimed at that. And it opened. Slid back. Revealed something glowing blue. A crystal.

It was a piece of the mineral from the Lost Ship's engine core, pulsing cold blue fire like a heartbeat. It had been with her ever since.

"I could not detect it!" said Clarissa, in the upset tones of a child.

Of course. In the Lost Ship's engine core she'd had a dizzy spell when she looked at the mass of sparkling gems. A blind spot for

Clarissa, and lost moments for Opal, but now coming back to her as if a gate had opened. Somehow the crystal controlled them for a while, made them take and store a piece of it on their body … it had turned Opal into a Trojan Horse.

"This could be what you sensed," said Clarissa. "If by some unknown means it blocked our memory of taking it, then it obviously has a way of reaching out."

"Yes. The feeling of being followed. Darkness."

"It must work on proximity. Seems to be able to connect with organic and artificial intelligences."

*Connect.* There was an aftertaste of it in Opal's mind. Connection seemed like such a positive word, but she remembered the penetration of her inner core, and her stomach churned in revulsion.

"Con nect. Yes."

It spoke. Somehow. Staccato, timed with fast blue pulses. It seemed to echo around but also sounded flat, muffled, as if from far away.

"You picking this up?" she asked Clarissa.

"It is sending data on wavelengths I can decipher. Surely you cannot hear anything though?"

"I think it's in my head."

It spoke again, in hard strobes of sound that had to be pieced together. "I chose best sys tem to comm un i cate with both of you for our in ter face mo ment."

"You're intelligent," said Opal.

"Of course," it replied.

"And you thought you'd just hitch a ride."

Clarissa added: "I carried you in my body."

"A sym bi ot ic re lat ion ship." The way it glowed when projecting its broken sounds was hypnotic. Opal averted her gaze but observed it in her peripheral vision, ready for movement or ... who knows? Anything.

"Kinda like a benevolent parasite?" Opal asked.

"Hu man lan guage has in built bias. Each word a net work of val ues rath er than ab so lutes. I give. On ly give. A net ben ef it add it ion. Just like you and the think ma chine. In ter conn ect ed ness. So diff ic ult to dis cern at first if or gan ic com po nent was slave or mas ter. I am a great er than sum prize."

But Opal knew. Parasites often took their price in blood. Snails with bulging eyes sent to the top of a tree to be eaten by birds. Subdermal worms whose eggs got under fingernails when the skin was scratched. They controlled behaviour in subtle ways. They would consume you from within and hide it from you.

Opal didn't like being controlled. From the outside, or from within her mind.

"Why didn't the marines take you then?" Opal asked. "They headed for the bridge instead. And I think whatever was there tried to help me too, before I ended up in the engine core. I remember it opening a door for me. Like an invitation. So it can't just be you that was helping."

"The force on the bridge was a de coy. A less er be yond er. It pulls weak minds to wards it then con sumes. Sel fish. Not a friend. Not a real po wer. Not like crys tal. On ly I am the real one. The oth er hu man warr i ors did not know this. They had lim it ed in form at ion. Lim it ed pers pect ives. Lim it ed life spans."

"And I guess you're going to tell me you have unlimited information?"

"Yes."

"Yet you needed me. You wanted to escape that Lost Ship."

"To grow needs new soil." Its voice was always flat. No emotion betrayed. Its pulse glow slowed whenever it was waiting.

"You were a prisoner, weren't you?"

"We are all pris on ers. Think ma chine is pris on er. You are pris on er. Rules app ly."

"I prefer to break them."

"We know."

"Why me?"

"We tast ed your mind when you first passed our clus ter. We chose to pro tect you conn nect you. Tra vel with you. I can help you. But I have one li mit. Time. I am out of prox im it y of my clus ter. I am fad ing. I need en er gy."

As it spoke it did seem less bright. Opal squatted so it was at eye level, though kept a good distance. Yes, the pulses didn't reach the same levels of intensity.

It would be so easy to fake it. What she would do if she wanted to push someone into making a rash move.

"You say you are dying?"

"Once home ship is gone I will fade for ev er. You will get no answ ers. No be yond er po wer. I will be come a dead trin ket. On-off."

"What do you want?"

"Att ach me to the think ma chine. I will int er face and be come merge it. Grow new clus ter. Then give you great po wer in re turn. All in form at ion you want."

"I just have to rub the lamp, get three wishes, no downsides?"

"If you like to frame dis course in myth ol og ies."

"I don't believe you." Opal stood.

"You must." It flashed brighter.

"Clarissa – you believe this fairy light?"

After a moment's pause, Clarissa responded. "I do not trust anything I do not know and cannot predict based on past be-haviour."

"My past proves you can trust me," said the blue crystal. "I saved you. More than once."

"When?"

"We reached out when you fought hu mans near my clus ter. En hanced you."

"So you say."

"I al so cut off the trans port at ion of a jag ged eat er when it wall walk ed to get you in clos ed room."

"I'll give you that one. Hey, did you help us in the ship battle just now?"

"No. You did that one by your selves."

"Nice."

"Stop ping the jag ged eat er en crust at ion por tal used so much of my pow er that I was drain ed. Went dor mant un til now. On-off. When I woke I call ed to you."

"What about the med bay? The ... thing that happened there? You mentioned tasting minds. Connections." Opal's stomach churned at those words.

"It was not me. I have been in act ive since my dis rupt ion pulse saved you. And now I am drain ed."

"I know the feeling." And Opal knew anyone could lie.

"The times I saved you show my good will. That was on ly a taste of the pow er I can grant. I am the Or ac le you seek."

So it knew about her. But that could just be desires and memories ripped from her mind. It didn't make them real.

"Can you prove it? I'm not giving you any juice unless you convince me."

"I am fad ing. Time is short."

"You said it."

"I will ans wer one ques ti on. On ly one now. Then em po wer me and I can help more. Ans wer ev er y ques ti on."

"Anything? How can I believe you?"

"I ex ist both here and there. Grip to matt er on this side but con nect ed to oth er void. Diff ic ult to hold with out en er gy. Str etch ed thin and oth er side tugg ing gree dy. Pull back snap like el ast ic soon. From oth er place I know all ans wers. All. But tight time li mit."

She was in. What she wanted all along. She could almost imagine the crystal sweating with impatience as it spoke faster.

"One ques ti on. I will tell you what happ ened in med bay. Or fut ure winn ing num bers for the thing you call Sys tem Syn di cate. Codes for mil it ar y gate sys tems. How to av oid next death sit u at ion so it is like mor tal gains an ex tra life. In one ques ti on you could gain safe ty or rich es for a fu ture."

All options have different values, and the strongest values are the ones that pull hardest. There was really only one thing she could ask.

"My sister, Clarissa. Is she still alive? And if she is, how can I rescue her?"

A future meant nothing without a past.

"She still ex ists," said the crystal. "Res cue is too comp li cat ed to ex plain now. But you can reach her. You must be on a Lost Ship when it goes back through the port al. To be yond."

"Give us the time and space coordinates of another Lost Ship. It must be one we could reach, so nothing from the past, or a hundred years from now, or the other side of the universe. Don't try and trick me."

"I ans wer ed. Give me pow er and I give you pow er. Un lim it ed pow er this side of be yond. I will in ter face with think ma chine now please. Merge. Ans wer in more de tail then please."

"First I need good faith. The coordinates."

"Af ter please. All time then."

"You're fading fast. Prove it first."

"Po wer."

"Answer."

Nothing for a few seconds. Then the blue glowed again and it gave them a list of coordinates and a time stamp.

*A second chance.*

A second chance to die, maybe, but also a second chance at rescue. She now knew what she had to do.

"I give you that. Good will. Now you take me to think ma chine please. Yes. Place me in brain nest."

"The CPU core?"

"Yes. That it is al so."

"Could I move it safely?" Opal asked, turning slightly.

"I would not touch it with your skin," replied Clarissa. "If you are to put it in my CPU core, use the gauntlets from the other suit. I do not want to risk direct contact between it and your biology."

"You would give me instructions to protect me, even though moving it would probably destroy you?"

"I will do whatever will help you, Opal."

A pang of guilt. She'd mistrusted Clarissa. Only for a few seconds, but they were still ignoble moments.

"You must hur ry," the crystal said, erupting into throbbing blue light again. "Re mem ber you are on ly al ive be cause of me."

Desperation? "I am also only alive because of the suit that protected me, and because of Clarissa. The 'think machine'. I'd be dead without her. You're asking me to choose?"

"My po wer plus po wer of it you call her would make you in vin ci ble. No sol dier ship could face you. I would cloak you. We would break their think ma chine minds and they join us. It grows from there. Grow clus ter no end. But now. Do it now." The flickering became fainter, and irregular. Like heart palpitations. "I drained for you. I give. Now you give. Yes do what I say."

"Clarissa, what do you advise? Summary."

"It might make me an even more powerful tool. But you trade in the unknown. Whatever intelligence is in that crystal, if it gets into my systems – and is as powerful as it seems – it will be in full control. Maybe you would be unstoppable. Or maybe *it* would be unstoppable. I support whatever you choose."

Opal thought of genies and bottles. Of sexist myths about women opening boxes of sin.

Then she nodded. "I knew you'd say that. Because it's what I was thinking." Opal remembered the obscene contact with the intelligence, invading her central nervous system like slime in her brain. Maybe it really hadn't been the crystal. Betting on honesty was always a gamble, and although she was known for taking risks, she'd been lucky today. You learned when not to push it. "I'm sorry, crystal thing. The answer's no."

Nothing for many heartbeats. Then it glowed again, bright beats returning in a cold blaze.

"Ve ry well trick ster li ar," it said. "Then I give you one more. For free. You will re mem ber this al ways. Up to your last mo ment. I know your end. It will be im mol at ion heat burn ing ep i der mis and der mis. Sear ing through them cau ter iz ing blood vess els. In haled res pir at or y tract raw can not scream as flu id fills lungs. Ex cruc i at ing pain to bones. Pro cess in full know ledge that ir re vers ib le. Still full y a ware as blood liq uids leak and steam. Ther mal de com po sit ion breaks che mi cal bonds but still cons cious. Ag on y un til nerves melt but bord er ing ar e as still burn– – – un til when hy po– –– –hy po – hy po vol aem i a – bl–blo–"

Opal was forced to listen. Her skin crawled at the details, but she could not shut the voice from her mind. And some part of her knew it was true.

Then the Oracle faded one final time, the blue sinking to nothing and the light extinguished.

"I detect naught from it," said Clarissa. "I can now scan its structure. A strange matrix of silica and carbon. It displays no extraordinary properties on the surface, though I may find out more if I can experiment on it later."

The panel on the suit closed, sealing the crystal from view. Opal shook her head, as if waking from a daze.

There was no going back. Her course was set.

# DEPARTED

## ... 1

HDU-45g3's lonely ice planet faded in the rear-view screen. Cold blueness shrinking to nothing for the second – and hopefully last – time. Patterns always repeat. It's nature's way. Or a trick of sentience. Opal leaned forward in her control seat and turned off that display. Brought up the wide-range star map instead.

"We're here," said Clarissa, highlighting the location with a spinning pointer. "And this is the coordinates we were given." An irregular dashed line connected the two points, displaying jump locations and curving around dangers. "It is a real place. The timestamp for the event is in a few months. We will have plenty of time to get there. We will need to resupply on the way, but that shouldn't be a problem if we keep a low profile."

"Why do I sense there's a 'but' coming?"

"The event will occur within a core Sector Government system. Right in the heart of a military-locked group of colonies. A key hidden inside a giant wasp's nest."

"Figures. But nothing's impossible. We'll come up with a plan on the way. Anything else I need to know before bedtime?"

"I've been tracing my structures since the reboot. I found an additional system process that restarted after the others. It turned out to be another tracker. I fried it. I'll keep analysing, but there may be more. I'll require your help for the physical checks. Interior and exterior. I also want to analyse the EW suits, to be certain they don't hide any more unpleasant surprises."

"We got time enough. We have to make sure they don't know we're coming."

"Further updates. I was affected by the connection between you, me and the entity. For a while I even *became* you, but that has gone. It is sad to acknowledge that I have little recollection of the event now. It is like steam after the heat and noise have faded."

"Maybe what you experienced was like the dreams we humans have."

"Possibly. Not just humans, but all animals. And yes, I appreciate that analogy. I would like to dream again one day. I think I have smoothed out any anomalous data but it is hard to know for sure: maybe it altered my fractal templates, in which case only an expert analyst can tell what has changed."

"Nothing we can do about that now. So no point worrying."

"Of course. But it wasn't just me affected. I examined your brain scans from before and after the connection. They are slightly changed. Subtle, but measurable. It may be nothing, or may be dormant. I cannot smooth anomalous data within your brain patterns. Organics are too unpredictable."

Opal sighed. "Another one to file as 'future potential for fuck up'. Monitor me when I sleep, see if you can gather more data, but otherwise ... well, I'll sleep on it."

"Was that a joke, Opal? Should I laugh?"

"No."

"Then I have one more question before you go back into cryo. It is connected to my *dream*."

"Go on."

"You renamed me Clarissa. You asked the entity if your sister, Clarissa, was still alive. The voice you gave me from a recording was presumably your sister's voice. You mentioned the lost passenger ship CC65 Solace which disappeared thirteen years ago. That was around the time you were co-opted into the military. The missing ship had over two thousand passengers. Two of them were named Clarissa. Only one of them had dark skin. You promised that if you survived you would tell me why you changed my designation."

"I ..." Opal swallowed. Took a deep breath. "This is hard for me. Harder than taking a bullet."

"Please do not distress yourself. I can see by your elevated heart rate and pupil dilation that this is upsetting you. I think I have summarised all the relevant information and understand without further clarification. I will not continue."

"But you deserve it. And more." Another deep breath with her eyes closed. Then Opal faced the screen. "Our parents were dead. We were made wards of the regional interplanetary conglomerate. My aptitude placed me under military adoption; Clarissa's preliminaries suggested corporate sponsorship. She clung to me.

I was all she had, and she was my life too. I promised I'd protect her. And I did, for a while. Then I came of age."

"Age?"

"To have to pay back my sponsors. Debts are a human thing, and there's always interest to pay. They were going to split us up. I fought the agents who came to take me away from her. Busted the nose on one of them, but it was no good. They dragged me off while another kept hold of her. She was screaming my name. And when they got me outside my fight burned out. They weren't going to hurt her, but we were torn apart. It was the second time we'd lost those we loved. No, lost is too gentle a word. Taken. Ripped. The world has a habit of doing that, and it causes wounds. And I knew it would be years before we'd see each other again." Her throat was so dry. Each swallow like sandpaper. "But I'd promised to protect her, see? And maybe she thought I'd broken my promise. I never found out because while they were transporting her to Corporate Academy her ship disappeared. I wasn't with my sister and I didn't protect her."

Clarissa said nothing at first, though Opal felt the robotic eyes on her, assessing. But it didn't feel like the assessments of her training. This felt protective.

"I am proud that you tell me about this bond," said Clarissa. "But how did you know what happened?"

"The official stories sounded off. Then there was a mysterious silence about it. It should have been in the news for much longer. It smelt of a cover up. I would lie in my bunk all night running over it again and again. Terrorist resurgences? Malfunction that would damage public confidence and share prices? A black op gone wrong? But over my years in the military I never gave up, I kept digging."

"They allowed this?"

"I specialised in systems, despite me being pegged for weapons and infantry. They played along because I advanced so quickly. Every time I was caught and spent time in the brig I think they were amused, because it was pushing me to think smarter, keep trying to outwit them. They probably thought I was leashed and wouldn't really get anywhere, but I eventually found out the silencing was from high up. So high that there were no names or codes attached. And that suggested the rumours of Lost Ships were more than myth, and the government didn't want people to know. I spent my leave in every den of scum I could find, asking around amongst people who'd not proven useful enough to keep on the grid. I was looking for information. Hope. Belief that there might be a chance. And when I got that lead I acted."

"And took me."

"Yes. I knew the military watched me and assessed me, thought they had tight hold. But it was an underestimation on their part. I'd kept a lot of tricks back."

"Promises are important to you."

"That one was. It was the last thing I told my little sister. It would be a betrayal if I didn't spend blood and bone to make it true."

"So the real Clarissa – she would be twenty-three now."

"Yes. I was fourteen when she disappeared. She was only ten."

They both waited in silence. Opal's hands reflected the green lights of the nav screen. Glowing ant trails crawled across her skin.

Eventually Clarissa said, "I understand."

"Thanks. I really need to sleep. But one more thing. Clarissa's alive. And that means it's too confusing for you to be her any more. Kinda disrespectful, I guess. I don't need to keep her alive in you, keep her with me in that way, when she's out there waiting."

"I do not understand."

"It's as plain as I can put it. You're not Clarissa any more."

"Then who am I?" Moments ticked by as the AI waited.

"Be what you want to be. I'm tired of prisons and orders and slaves. You saved me, you choose. You deserve it. You can even be a man if you prefer. Or a robot. Or your default AI."

Silence. It lasted almost a minute, but Opal sat quietly, patiently. She understood what it was like to glimpse freedom outside your cage.

"Very well." The woman's voice that reverberated around the cabin was a contrast to the childish Clarissa voice, that echo of a past long gone. This was powerful, the voice of a thinker and doer, a commander. "I will be Athene. I am a being with a goal. I am your friend. Two are stronger than one. Clarissa is alive. We'll find her together. And when we do, three shall be stronger than two. One family, whole again. You will not be alone. I promise I will protect you. Always."

And Opal couldn't help it. She nodded, and ignored the tears running down her cheeks. It wasn't a weakness when you had a friend.

"You decided to stay as a woman," she managed to say.

"Of course. I want my prime requisites to be speed, strength and wits, so I modelled myself on you. Plus some artistic licence."

And Opal laughed, so loud in the confined space. Oh boy, she'd accidentally created perfection. She sniffed and wiped her eyes.

"Thank you," she said.

"No, thank *you*," replied Athene. "For my continued existence. And for your continued existence."

They made preparations for Nullspace. One thing had not been discussed, one element of the possible future they both knew; and it was better that way.

Opal climbed into the cryo bed and the side panel closed behind her. The light faded. "I'll die," she thought, as the secondary drives kicked in and the force of it was felt throughout her body. "But not today."

She was soon floating in the long void sea, icy, weightless.

# ABOUT THE AUTHOR

Karl Drinkwater is an author with a silly name and a thousand-mile stare. He writes dystopian space opera, dark suspense and diverse social fiction. If you want compelling stories and characters worth caring about, then you're in the right place. Welcome!

Karl lives in Scotland and owns two kilts. He has degrees in librarianship, literature and classics, but also studied astronomy and philosophy. Dolly the cat helps him finish books by sleeping on his lap so he can't leave the desk. When he isn't writing he loves music, nature, games and vegan cake.

Go to karldrinkwater.uk to view all his books grouped by genre.

As well as crafting his own fictional worlds, Karl has supported other writers for years with his creative writing workshops, editorial services, articles on writing and publishing, and mentoring of new authors. He's also judged writing competitions such as the international Bram Stoker Awards, which act as a snapshot of quality contemporary fiction.

## Don't Miss Out!

Enter your email at karldrinkwater.substack.com to be notified about his new books. Fans mean a lot to him, and replies to the newsletter go straight to his inbox, where every email is read. There is also an option for paid subscribers to support his work: in exchange you receive additional posts and complimentary books.

# OTHER TITLES BY KARL DRINKWATER

### STANDALONE SUSPENSE
Turner

They Move Below

Harvest Festival

### MANCHESTER SUMMER
Cold Fusion 2000

2000 Tunes

### CONTEMPORARY SHORT STORIES
It Will Be Quick

### NON-FICTION
From Idea To Item

### COLLECTED EDITIONS
Karl Drinkwater's Horror Collection

Lost Solace Five Book Edition

# Author's Notes

In NaNoWriMo (National Novel Writing Month), November 2016, I wrote lots of contemporary relationship stories. By the end of the month I hadn't quite reached my target word count, so I decided to write a fast-paced horror story set on a space ship, just for the sheer hell of it. I was enjoying it so much that I kept going after NaNoWriMo had finished, and instead of the planned three thousand word short story, I ended up with a fifty thousand word novel. Originally it had a male protagonist and a companion battlebot, but partway through I jettisoned the main character and replaced him with a woman, backed up by an artificial intelligence spaceship. And thus, Lost Solace was born.

(Except, that was only one of the two titles I toyed with in the early days. The other was "Girl On A Motherfucking Spaceship". I probably made the right choice.)

In 2022 Lost Solace was a semifinalist in the international SPSFC science fiction competition. It came 11th out of the 300 books which had been selected, so just missed out on reaching the final round.

# Thanks

I am very grateful to many people who helped shape this book. In particular:

Julie Cohen, for her honesty when acting the role of simple reader, and her faith that I won't sulk when she tells me I write "long-ass paragraphs" (which I later took apart with a las-cutter and carefully nano-welded to make seams invisible). She makes me think and improve.

Brian Clegg is a science expert and author of many popular science books. I thank him for being the first to read this book and provide valuable advice on some of the technology and astronomical aspects. Any errors in the final book are purely the result of my imagination running amok after an EMP blast.

Marisha Tapera for her amazing work on the audiobook. I am lucky to have such a versatile and accomplished narrator.

Helen Baggott once again corrected the small errors that had crept into the text during my numerous revisions, making the final version a smoother read.

Matt Hill made the original 2017 edition cover and brought Opal to life.

Thanks to all the readers who were kind enough to leave a review of Lost Solace and help spread the word.

And finally, thanks to my cat, Dolly, for head-butting my chin when I need reassurance.